Warren Webster

Letter of the Secretary of War

Warren Webster

Letter of the Secretary of War

ISBN/EAN: 9783337213428

Printed in Europe, USA, Canada, Australia, Japan

Cover: Foto ©Raphael Reischuk / pixelio.de

More available books at **www.hansebooks.com**

LETTER

OF

THE SECRETARY OF WAR,

COMMUNICATING,

In answer to a resolution of the Senate of the 9th instant, copy of the proceedings of the general court-martial for the trial of Assistant Surgeon Webster; report of the general-in-chief of the army on the management of general hospitals; general orders in relation to the medical department, and general orders and instructions relating to hospitals.

FEBRUARY 25, 1864.—Read and referred to the Committee on Military Affairs and the Militia.
MARCH 1, 1864.—Ordered to be printed.

WAR DEPARTMENT,
Washington City, February 25, 1864.

SIR : In compliance with the resolution of the Senate, dated the 9th instant, I have the honor to transmit herewith the following documents :

1. Copy of proceedings of the general court-martial convened in New York city by virtue of Special Orders No. 118, December 7, 1863, for the trial of Assistant Surgeon Webster.

2. Report of the general-in-chief of the army on the subject of authority given military commanders over general hospitals.

3. General Orders No. 4, of 1847, No. 43, of 1862, and No. 53, of 1862, containing acts of Congress in relation to the medical department.

4. General Orders Nos. 36, 65, and 78, of 1862, and No. 308, of 1863, containing regulations relating to hospitals.

5. Copies of letters conveying instructions in regard to hospitals, dated, respectively, January 28, 1863, August 5, 1863, December 31, 1863, and January 29, 1864.

I am, sir, very respectfully, your obedient servant,

EDWIN M. STANTON.
Secretary of War.

Hon. H. HAMLIN,
President of the Senate.

PROCEEDINGS OF A GENERAL COURT-MARTIAL CONVENED AT NEW YORK CITY PER SPECIAL ORDER NO. 118, OF DECEMBER 7, 1863, HEADQUARTERS DEPARTMENT OF THE EAST.

Major F. T. Dent, 4th infantry, president; Captain R. T. Frank, 8th infantry, judge advocate.

Prisoner tried, Assistant Surgeon Warren Webster, United States army.

Official copy of the trial of Assistant Surgeon Warren Webster, United States army, for the use of United States Senate.

J. HOLT,
Judge Advocate General.

Proceedings of a general court-martial convened at New York city by virtue of the following order, viz:

Special Orders, }   HEADQUARTERS DEPARTMENT OF THE EAST,
No. 118.   }   *New York City, December* 7, 1863.

A general court-martial is hereby appointed to meet at New York city on the 10th day of December, 1863, at 10 o'clock a. m., or as soon thereafter as practicable, for the trial of such persons as may be brought before it by authority from these headquarters.

Detail for the court:

Major F. T. Dent, 4th United States infantry.
Captain William Clinton, 10th United States infantry.
Captain David P. Hancock, 7th United States infantry.
Captain Wright Rives, additional aide-de-camp.
Thomas Lord, jr., aide-de-camp.
First Lieutenant Samuel T. Crowley, 4th United States infantry.
First Lieutenant Clarence M. Bailey, 6th United States infantry.
Captain Royal T. Frank, 8th United States infantry, judge advocate.

No others officers than those named can be assembled without manifest injury to the service.

Should any of the officers named in the detail be unable to attend, the court will, nevertheless, proceed to and continue the business before it, provided the number present be not less than the minimum prescribed by law.

By command of Major General Dix.

D. T. VAN BUREN,
Assistant Adjutant General.

GENERAL COURT-MARTIAL ROOMS,
New York City, December 14, 1863.

The court met pursuant to the above orders, which having been read by the judge advocate, and the roll called, the following members were present:

Major F. T. Dent, 4th United States infantry.
Captain William Clinton, 10th United States infantry.
Captain David P. Hancock, 7th United States infantry.
First Lieutenant Samuel T. Crowley, 4th United States infantry.
First Lieutenant Clarence M. Bailey, 6th United States infantry.
Captain Royal T. Frank, 8th United States infantry, judge advocate.

Absent:

Captain Wright Rives, additional aide-de-camp.
Captain Thomas Lord, aide-de-camp.

The judge advocate here applied to the court for authority to employ a recording clerk, at one dollar per day, which was granted.

The case of Assistant Surgeon Warren Webster not being prepared for trial, the court adjourned to meet on Wednesday, the 16th instant, at 10½ o'clock a. m.

R. T. FRANK,
Captain 8th Infantry and Judge Advocate.

Proceedings of a general court-martial convened at New York city by virtue of the following order, viz:

Special Orders,　　HEADQUARTERS DEPARTMENT OF THE EAST,
No. 118.　　　　*New York City, December* 7, 1863.

A general court-martial is hereby appointed to meet at New York city on the 10th day of December, 1863, at 10 o'clock a. m., or as soon thereafter as practicable, for the trial of such persons as may be brought before it by authority from these headquarters.

Detail for the court :

Major F. T. Dent, 4th United States infantry.
Captain William Clinton, 10th United States infantry.
Captain David P. Hancock, 7th United States infantry.
Captain Wright Rives, additional aide-de-camp.
Captain Thomas Lord, jr., aide-de-camp.
First Lieutenant Samuel T. Crowley, 4th United States infantry.
First Lieutenant Clarence M. Bailey, 6th United States infantry.
Captain Royal T. Frank, 8th United States infantry, judge advocate.

No other officers than those named can be assembled without manifest injury to the service.

Should any of the officers named in the detail be unable to attend, the court will, nevertheless, proceed to and continue the business before it, provided the number present be not less than the minimum prescribed by law.

By command of Major General Dix.
D. T. VAN BUREN,
Assistant Adjutant General.

GENERAL COURT-MARTIAL ROOMS,
New York City, December 16, 1863.

The court met pursuant to the above order and adjournment.

Present:

Major F. T. Dent, 4th United States infantry.
Captain William Clinton, 10th United States infantry.
Captain David P. Hancock, 7th United States infantry.
Captain Wright Rives, additional aide-de-camp.
Captain Thomas Lord, jr., additional aide-de-camp.
First Lieutenant Samuel T. Crowley, 4th United States infantry.
First Lieutenant Clarence M. Bailey, 6th United States infantry.
Captain Royal T. Frank, 8th United States infantry, judge advocate.

The proceedings of the previous day having been read were approved by the court.

The court then proceeded to the trial of Assistant Surgeon Warren Webster, United States army, who, being brought into court, and having heard the foregoing order read, was asked if he had any objection to any member named in the order, to which he replied in the negative.

The court was then duly sworn by the judge advocate, and the judge advocate by the presiding officer, in the presence of the accused, and Assistant Surgeon Warren Webster, United States army, was arraigned under the following charges and specifications:

CHARGE 1ST.—*Disobedience of orders.*

Specification.—In this: that he, the said Warren Webster, assistant surgeon United States army, in charge of the McDougall general hospital, having received an order from Brigadier General Canby, commanding the city and harbor of New York, (through Brigadier General Brown, commanding Fort Schuyler,) based upon an order from the War Department (which said order accompanied the order of Brigadier General Canby, and was read by Surgeon Webster) to arrest and send to Fort Columbus Private Phillip Fitzsimmons, of company F, 40th regiment New York volunteers, a deserter and an inmate of his hospital, did refuse to obey the said order. All this at or near Fort Schuyler, New York, between the 10th and 15th of November, 1863.

CHARGE 2D.—*Conduct prejudicial to good order and military discipline.*

Specification.—In this: that he, the said Warren Webster, assistant surgeon United States army, in charge of the McDougall general hospital, having refused to arrest and send to Fort Columbus Private Phillip Fitzsimmons, of company F, 40th New York volunteers, did then have presented to him by Captain Hannam an order from Brigadier General Brown, commanding Fort Schuyler, directing him, the said Captain Hannam, to repair to the McDougall general hospital and arrest Private Phillip Fitzsimmons, of company F, 40th New York volunteers, did forbid the said Captain Hannam to enter any ward of his hospital, and did also fail to give him any assistance in carrying out the orders of Brigadier General Brown. All this at or near Fort Schuyler on or about the 15th November, 1863.

To which charges and specifications the accused pleaded as follows:
To the specification, first charge, not guilty.
To the first charge, not guilty.
To the specification, second charge, guilty.
To the second charge, not guilty.

Brigadier General Harvey Brown, United States army, a witness for the prosecution, being duly sworn, says: On or about the 12th day of November I received the descriptive roll of Private Fitzsimmons with indorsements, so far as I remember, by the Adjutant General at Washington, directing the man to be apprehended. On an envelope, department headquarters, New York city and harbor, was an order directing me to have the man arrested and sent to Fort Columbus. The man being at the McDougall hospital, which was in charge of Dr. Webster, and within the precincts of my command, I sent all the papers to Dr. Webster with an order for him to carry the order of General Canby into execution.

On or about the 14th of November I received a communication from Dr. Webster of about the following purport: "That considering general hospitals to be under the sole control of the Surgeon General of the army, he considered himself bound to obey orders relating to the transfer of patients from the hospital only when coming through the Surgeon General, or his representative, the medical director, Dr. McDougall. Dr. Webster about this time had been thrown from his horse, and was confined to his room, and I believe to his bed. Desirous of avoiding trouble, which I saw might arise from the doctor's refusal to obey order, I went to his quarters and urged him to withdraw his refusal, and stated to him, that if having done so, he would state to me that he considered the man unfit to be removed, I would take no further action in the case, but would refer the whole subject back to department headquarters for further instructions; that otherwise, the order being imperative, I should take the man by force, if necessary, from the hospital.

He declined to say anything in regard to the man whatever, whether he was well or sick, and also refused to withdraw his letter refusing to obey the order or to deliver up the man. After some further conversation, I told him that I should send a guard to take the man. He desired me to delay the execution of the order for one hour, which I told him I would do, and left him. I returned to the fort, (the hospital being contiguous to the fort,) and gave Captain Hannau, officer of the day, written orders to take a guard, and also some men, if necessary, to carry the soldier; to go to McDougall hospital, and to report to Dr. Webster, and to show him the order.

If Dr. Webster turned over the man, to bring him to the fort, and if not, to ascertain where he was, and to bring him forcibly, if necessary. Not knowing the condition of the man, I directed Dr. Peas, the post surgeon, to accompany Captain Hannan, and to see that the removal of the man was done with as little prejudice to his health as possible. The man was brought to the post hospital by Captain Hannan, and was sent by my order the next morning to Fort Columbus.

Question by the judge advocate. State if you recognize this paper, and when and under what circumstances you first saw it. (The paper was here shown to the witness.)

Answer. I recognize the paper as the original order which I received from General Canby. It was around the descriptive roll to Fitzsimmons.

The paper is appended (above) to the proceedings, and marked A.

Question by judge advocate. Is this the original paper which you sent to Dr. Webster? (The paper was here shown to the witness.)

Answer. It is. The indorsement referred to is that of General Canby. The paper is here appended, and marked B.

Question by judge advocate. What paper is this? (The paper was here shown to the witness.)

Answer. This is the original paper which Dr. Webster returned to me, refusing to deliver up the man. The paper is appended, and marked C.

Question by judge advocate. Do you recognize this paper? (The paper was here shown to the witness.)

Answer. This is the original order I gave to Captain Hannan. The paper is appended, and marked D.

Question by accused. How long have you known the accused?

Answer. Some six months.

Question by accused. Please state, excluding the occurrences covered by the present charge and specifications, if you have found the accused, in your official intercourse with him, respectful and courteous, or otherwise?

Answer. Decidedly courteous and respectful.

Question by accused. Have you found him captious or disposed to give annoyance to yourself?

Answer. Not at all.

Question by accused. If you consider yourself familiar with the management of the McDougall general hospital, will you please state your opinion of the manner in which the accused has administered that hospital while under his charge?

Answer. The management of that hospital has come under my daily observation. I consider that Dr. Webster has administered the department with much ability.

Question by accused. Is not the McDougall general hospital entirely distinct from the post hospital under your command?

Answer. It is. I will state that everything that appertains to the exterior management of the McDougall hospital is, by order of General Canby, under my charge, the same as the rest of the post, but the interior management of it is under the charge of the medical officer in charge of the hospital.

Question by accused. Will you please state what, so far as relates to being under your command, is, in your opinion, the military distinction between your post hospital and the McDougall general hospital?

Answer. I do not conceive that I have anything to do with the reception or dismissal of the patients of the McDougall hospital, or their treatment. Everything appertaining to the exterior management, relative to the guards, to the passes, &c., is under my charge. I consider Dr. Webster as much obliged to obey my orders as any of the officers of my post. Orders from the Adjutant General's office, both at Washington and here, pass through me, and I communicate them to Dr. Webster. The orders from the medical department never pass through my hands, but are sent directly to the surgeon in charge. Dr. Webster makes no reports to me, and no reports of or from the general hospital are made to the post.

Question by accused. Has the name of the accused been borne on your post returns since he has been in charge of the McDougall general hospital?

Answer. He has not; nor any of his officers.

Question by accused. Why did you order the accused to arrest and send to Fort Columbus Private Fitzsimmons, instead of ordering your adjutant, or some officer under your command, to do so?

Answer. I did, because Dr. Webster was the immediate commander of Fitzsimmons. All orders should pass through the next superior.

Question by accused. Is there not a well-understood distinction in this department, between Fort Schuyler, as a post, and the McDougall hospital?

Answer. There is a decided distinction. I consider the reason why the McDougall hospital has been put, in any manner, under my control, is because it is within the precincts of Fort Schuyler; and there can be but one commanding officer at a post. The manner in which a commanding officer would exercise his authoriity in this particular is a matter of discretion with him, and for which he is responsible.

Question by accused. Is Private Fitzsimmons described in the letter of his colonel, in the indorsement of the Provost Marshal General, or in the order of General Canby, as being at the McDougall general hospital?

Answer. I think not. He is described, so far as I remember, as being at Fort Schuyler. That is the uniform practice. Soldiers at the post or in that hospital are described as being at Fort Schuyler.

Question by accused. Please state whether, while you were commanding in the city and harbor of New York, you received orders, or intimation in any form, direct or indirect, from Major General Wool, the department commander, not to give orders to surgeons in charge of general hospitals, without reference to the medical director of the department?

Answer. I have no recollection of ever having received such an order.

Question by accused. Please state whether, while you were commanding in the city and harbor of New York, and General Wool was department commander, you issued orders directly to the surgeon in charge of the McDougall general hospital relating to the internal management of that hospital, or the transfer of patients to or from it?

Answer. I considered, when I commanded here, that all the hospitals in the city and harbor were all under my command, and, as I understand, I had that authority expressly from Washington. I, however, seldom interfered, as I considered the medical department the best judges in such cases. I have given Dr. Webster's predecessor orders, but whether it was before or after General Wool came here I cannot remember.

Question by accused. Did you state by letter to the accused, on or about October 6, 1863, that you would not in any manner interfere with the internal relations of the McDougall general hospital, and that you only claimed the right to post sentinels on the borders of the peninsula on which the hospital stands; and if so, do you recognize the copy of that letter, which I now submit, to be correct?

Answer. I did state that I would not interfere with the internal relations of the hospital, but I did not state that I only claimed a right to station sentinels on the borders of the peninsula. I recognize this paper to be a copy of a letter which I addressed to the accused.—(See letter marked "E," appended.)

The court here adjourned to meet at 10½ o'clock to-morrow morning.

R. T. FRANK,
Captain 8th Infantry, Judge Advocate.

GENERAL COURT-MARTIAL ROOMS,
New York City, December 17, 1863.

The court met pursuant to adjournment.

Present:

Major F. T. Dent, 4th United States infantry.
Captain William Clinton, 10th United States infantry.
Captain David P. Hancock, 7th United States infantry.
Captain Wright Rives, additional aide-de-camp.
Captain Thomas Lord, jr., aide-de-camp.
1st Lieutenant Samuel T. Crowley, 4th United States infantry.
1st Lieutenant Clarence M. Bailey, 6th United States infantry.
Captain R. T. Frank, 8th United States infantry, judge advocate.
The accused also present.

Yesterday's proceedings having been read were approved by the court.

Lieutenant J. I. Marcey, 10th U. S. infantry, a witness for the prosecution, being duly sworn, says:

Question by judge advocate. What is your official position?
Answer. I am provost marshal of Fort Columbus.
Question by judge advocate. Did you have turned over to your charge one Private Fitzsimmons, 40th New York volunteers; and if so, by whose order, from what place, and in what character?
Answer. He was turned over to me as a deserter from Fort Schuyler, by order of General Brown.
Question by judge advocate. Did you receive the descriptive roll of Fitzsimmons at that time?
Answer. I think I did, but am not positive.
Question by judge advocate. What disposition has been made of this descriptive roll?
Answer. The papers which I received with the prisoner were forwarded to the headquarters United States troops, city and harbor of New York.
Question by judge advocate. Was Fitzsimmons reported on these papers as a deserter?
Answer. He was.
Question by accused. By whom was Private Fitzsimmons mentioned as a deserter, on the papers that accompanied him, when he was turned over to you?
Answer. By the commanding officer of his regiment; I think it was in an indorsement on a letter from the surgeon at Fort Schuyler asking for his descriptive roll.
Question by accused. Did General Brown, in his order turning Fitzsimmons over to you, make any references to the physical condition of the man; and if so, what reference?
Answer. I do not think he did.
Question by the court. Have you received a communication from General Brown, and what was it?
Answer. I have in my office a communication from General Brown, with regard to the physical condition of the man, which, I think, was addressed by him to General Canby, and referred by him to Colonel Loomis, and by him to

me. I think it was to the effect that the man might be removed to Fort Columbus, but not to his regiment until he was better.

The prosecution here closed.

The accused, having been put on his defence, submitted in evidence General Orders No. 36 and 308, dated War Department, Adjutant General's office, Washington, April 7, 1862, and September 12, 1863. They are appended, and marked "F" and "G."

Surgeon William J. Sloan, United States army, a witness for the defence, being duly sworn, says:

Question by accused. What is your position at present in the military service, and how long have you discharged your present duties?

Answer. I am a surgeon in the army; I have been in the service almost 27 years.

Question by accused. How long have you known the accused?

Answer. I have known him since the fall of 1860. I first met him at Fort Larned, Pawnee Fork, and since he has been on duty in this department.

Question by accused. What has been your position while on duty in this department recently?

Answer. I am on duty in the medical director's office, principally in charge of the correspondence and the executive duties. I was formerly on duty as medical director, and had charge of the building of all the general hospitals in this harbor in 1862.

Question by accused. Please state what, so far as you have had the opportunity of judging, has been the character of the accused as an officer, whether obedient and respectful to his superiors, or otherwise. What is your opinion of the management of the McDougall general hospital by the accused, and what opportunity have you had of forming an opinion?

Answer. Dr. Webster stands high in the corps professionally. His character is that of a highly honorable gentleman, courteous, subordinate, and of first rate administrative ability. He has conducted the affairs of the McDougall hospital with great ability, as shown by the records and inspections. I have not had many opportunities of judging from personal inspection, though I have made several. That is not a part of my duty. I know that the medical director's opinion coincides with my own, and he makes inspections frequently. One of the best tests as to the manner in which this hospital is managed is the few complaints of the people at large made at our office.

Question by accused. Please state whether or not there is a well-understood distinction in the military orders and correspondence of this department between Fort Schuyler and the McDougall general hospital?

Answer. There is, and always has been. In the original instructions to me to erect a hospital in that vicinity, I was directed to go beyond the fort and glacis, and erect it on the grounds belonging to the United States.

Question by accused. Was not the ground upon which the hospital was erected considered at that time as beyond the precincts of the fort, and entirely separate from it?

Answer. I thought so.

Question by accused. Please state whether or not there is in the service a well-understood distinction between the post hospital at Fort Schuyler and the McDougall general hospital?

Answer. They are entirely distinct, and under different regulations.

Question by accused. Do you know of an indorsement in respect to the relations existing between the McDougall general hospital and the post at Fort Schuyler, dated October 2, 1863. Have you that indorsement; and if yea, will you produce it or a copy?

Answer. I do; and here produce a copy. (The paper is appended to the proceedings, and marked "II.")

Question by accused. Do you know of an indorsement by Major General Halleck in respect to the control to be exercised over general hospitals by subordinate military commanders, dated October 6, 1863. Have you a copy of so much of that indorsement as relates to general hospitals; and if yea, will you produce it?

Answer. I have a copy, and here produce it. (The copy is appended to the proceedings, and marked "I.")

Question by accused. Do you know of an indorsement by the Surgeon General, dated August 13, 1863, in respect to the control of military commanders over general hospitals? If yea, then will you produce that indorsement, or a copy of so much of it as relates to general hospitals?

Answer. I have a copy, and submit it. (It is appended, and marked "J.")

Question by accused. Please state whether or not the custom of the service in this department does not require that an order like that given to the accused, in relation to Private Fitzsimmons, should go through the medical director's office?

Answer. It has been the custom in regard to patients in general hospitals, but not to post hospitals. The commanding general of the department, particularly, sends orders that way. All papers referring to men in general hospitals are referred by the general commanding the department through the medical director to the surgeon in charge of the hospital, and all replies to such papers come back to the medical director and are transmitted by him to the general commanding the department. The medical director is on the staff of the general commanding the department.

Question by accused. Please state, so far as your experience goes, what has been the custom of Provost Marshal General Fry in transmitting orders directing the transfer of patients from general hospitals in this department. Have such orders been sent through the medical director?

Answer. I have no recollection of any order of that kind.

Question by accused. What course do you judge Provost Marshal General Fry would take in such a case, from what you know of the official correspondence of that office?

Answer. It is my opinion that if he had wanted a man arrested that was in a general hospital, that he would have sent the order through the medical director. As he did not do so, I think he must have been mistaken as to the whereabouts of the man. This is a mere opinion.

Question by accused. Are soldiers in McDougall general hospital generally described in orders and official papers as being at Fort Schuyler or at McDougall general hospital?

Answer. At the McDougall general hospital. Fort Schuyler is also mentioned to designate the particular point where the hospital is.

Question by accused. Have you, in your experience as assistant to the medical director in this department, known an order by superior military authority directing the transfer of a patient from a general hospital which did not contain the words "if able to travel?"

Answer. That is the invariable rule, even when coming from the Secretary of War, though there may have been some exceptions.

Question by accused. According to the custom of the service, have subordinate military commanders any control in the internal management of general hospitals or the discharge or transfer of patients?

Answer. I think not by recent decision. I mean by subordinate commanders, all those subordinate to the general commanding the department. The military commander has authority to discharge a man from service upon a surgeon's certificate of disability by order No. 36, 1862.

The court here adjourned to meet at 10½ o'clock to-morrow morning.

R. T. FRANK,
Captain 8th Infantry, Judge Advocate.

GENERAL COURT-MARTIAL ROOMS,
New York City, December 18, 1863.

The court met pursuant to adjournment.

Present:

Major F. T. Dent, 4th United States infantry.
Captain William Clinton, 10th United States infantry.
Captain David P. Hancock, 7th United States infantry.
Captain Wright Rives, additional aide-de-camp.
Captain Thomas Lord, jr., aide-de-camp.
First Lieutenant Samuel T. Crowley, 4th United States infantry.
First Lieutenant Clarence M. Bailey, 6th United States infantry.
Captain R. F. Frank, 8th United States infantry, judge advocate.

The accused also present.

The proceedings of yesterday having been read were approved by the court.

Surgeon William J. Sloan, witness for the defence—evidence continued.

Question by accused. State whether Private Fitzsimmons, 40th New York volunteers, was among patients ordered to be transferred in October last from general hospital, Governor's island, to the McDougall general hospital, and whether he was transferred.

Answer. He was ordered to be transferred on the 14th of October, and was transferred on the 16th.

Question by accused. Was he a patient in general hospital at Governor's island before being transferred to the McDougall hospital?

Answer. He was.

Question by accused. State what effect upon the discipline and efficiency of the general hospitals of this department the direct interference in their management of subordinate military commanders has had.

Answer. It has been the source of great trouble and controversy, and sometimes contradict the regulations adopted by the medical department. All the general hospitals in this department are governed by certain regulations and instructions. Interference with those regulations without the knowledge of the medical director has caused a great deal of trouble and annoyance.

Question by judge advocate. Was or was not the McDougall general hospital erected on the reservation of Fort Schuyler?

Answer. I do not know what the reservation was, but it was erected on the public grounds at Fort Schuyler, on the neck.

Question by judge advocate. Were not these grounds under the charge or command of the commanding officer of Fort Schuyler when the hospital was erected?

Answer. No. There was no commanding officer there at the time, and no troops.

(A paper was here submitted in evidence from Surgeon McDougall, medical director, the authenticity of the signature being admitted by the accused. The paper is appended, and marked "K.")

Question by court. You state (as a matter of opinion) the course Provost Marshal General Fry would pursue. State whether (as your opinion) this course would be from the constraint of existing orders, regulations, and instructions, or from the dictates of official courtesy.

Answer. All combined. I gave my opinion as an inference from the correspondence with the Provost Marshal General, now in our office.

Question by court. State whether, under existing orders, regulations and instructions, the general commanding the United States troops in the city and harbor of New York can remove by order a soldier undergoing treatment in any general hospital from that hospital without sending the order through the medical director?

Answer. He can do so. He takes the responsibility.

Question by court. Would not such an order be as imperative sent through the Adjutant General's department, as when sent through the medical director?

Answer. It would, but I hardly think it would be courteous to the general commanding the department to take a man from his command without his knowledge.

Question by court. What is, from existing orders, instructions and regulations, the extent of the command of the general commanding the United States troops in the city and harbor of New York? Does it embrace the general hospitals in the city and vicinity of the harbor?

Answer. To a certain extent it does. The control and management of the hospitals and the patients rests with the medical department.

Assistant Surgeon E. H. Abadie, United States army, a witness for the defence, being duly sworn, says:

Question by accused. What is your position in the military service, and how long have you been in the army?

Answer. I am surgeon in the United States army; I entered the service in 1836; twenty-seven years in the service.

Question by accused. How long have you known the accused? Please state if he has been on duty with you; and if yea, when and where.

Answer. Dr. Webster was ordered to report to me for duty, to assist in establishing a hospital in Washington, early in December, 1861. From that time until the latter part of June, 1862, he remained on duty under me at the Douglas hospital.

Question by accused. State your opinion of the accused as a medical officer, and particularly whether you found him respectful and obedient to his superiors, or otherwise.

Answer. I have the highest opinion of the doctor's qualifications as a medical officer; and the manner of performing his duties, the whole time that he served with me, I ever found him prompt and attentive to his duties, invariably subordinate to all authority over him; in fact, unusually so.

Question by accused. Please state whether a wound rendered necessary by the surgical operation of removing a portion of the anterior and inferior surface of the clavicle, or collar-bone, which bone had been fractured by a musket ball, is of a dangerous character; and if so, for what reason?

Answer. The apex of the chest containing the lungs is closed immediately behind the seat of operation by a dense membrane from the neck and neighboring parts, strengthened by two loops, one on each side of the deep cervital fuscia, through which loop passes a tendon of a muscle which goes from the neck to the shoulder. These loops are attached immediately behind the articulation of the breast-bone and clavicle. This ceasing of the chest at this point sustains the whole weight of the atmosphere, and in case of destruction by inflammation or ulceration, or otherwise, would promptly destroy the patient's life. In addition to this, the danger of injuring the vessels that pass out of the chest to the neck and upper extremities. The sub-clavian, after passing out of the chest, ascends to pass over the first rib, just below the collar-bone, near the seat of the operation. The most important point to guard against in such an operation is to avoid accumulation and burrowing of matter that might endanger by pressure or inflammation the important parts described.

Question by accused. Please state whether, in your opinion, a soldier upon whom the operation just described has been performed would in fourteen days thereafter be in a fit state for removal from hospital?

Answer. Decidedly not. Granting that the operation had succeeded, and the case progressing favourably; exposure to the weather, accidental injury, too much exercise, might increase to a dangerous extent the inflammation already present essential to repair the surgical injury inflicted.

Acting Assistant Surgeon J. J. Caldwell, United States army, a witness for the defence, being duly sworn, says:

Question by accused. What is your position in the medical service of the army?

Answer. I am an acting assistant surgeon in the United States army, and on duty at the McDougall hospital.

Question by accused. Did you have under your treatment in the McDougall general hospital a patient named Private P. Fitzsimmons, company F, 40th regiment New York volunteers? If so, state how long he was under your treatment.

Answer. I have. He was under my treatment from the 15th October until the 15th of November, 1863.

Question by accused. What was his condition when received; was a surgical operation performed on him; if so, when? Please describe the operation.

Answer. When he came under my treatment he was suffering from a gunshot wound in the left breast and collar-bone or clavicle, with evidence of diseased or dead bone on the clavicle. A surgical operation was performed on the first of November, to remove this dead bone, making an incision of two inches and a half parallel with the clavicle or collar-bone, and deep enough to remove the dead portion of bone from the external surface, and under border of the clavicle.

Question by accused. Did you have charge of the ward in which Private Fitzsimmons was on November 15, 1863? If so, please state his condition on the morning of that day, and if you remember any other patient in that ward whose case was serious or critical enough to demand especial attention.

Answer. I did have charge of the ward in which Private Fitzsimmons was on November 15, 1863. On that morning the wound was still open and discharging pus, and had made very little progress towards healing, and there was evidence of the disease of the clavicle or collar-bone still progressing. I remember also the case of one John Fallens, a private of the 42d New York volunteers, who was then in a most critical state of health, suffering from a gunshot wound in the abdomen and intestines. His case was such as to demand strict repose, and absence from all disturbances likely to cause him any excitement.

Question by accused. Were Privates Fallen and Fitzsimmons in the same ward of the hospital?

Answer. They were.

Question by accused. Did you make any written report to the accused of the condition of these two men; and if so, will you produce a copy of it?

Answer. I did, and here produce the original report. (It is appended, and marked "L.")

The court here adjourned to meet at 10½ o'clock to-morrow morning.

R. T. FRANK,
Captain 8th Infantry, Judge Advocate.

GENERAL COURT-MARTIAL ROOMS,
New York City, December 19, 1863.

The court met pursuant to adjournment.

Present:

Major F. T. Dent, 4th United States infantry.
Captain William Clinton, 10th United States infantry.

Captain Wright Rives, additional aide-de-camp.
Captain Thomas Lord, jr., aide-de-camp.
First Lieutenant Samuel T. Crowley, 4th United States infantry.
The judge advocate and the accused also present.

Absent:
Captain David P. Hancock, 7th United States infantry.
First Lieutenant Clarence M. Bailey, 6th United States infantry.

The proceedings of the previous day having been read were approved by the court.

Captain Hancock and Lieutenant Bailey having arrived, resumed their seats.

Brigadier General Harvey Brown, United States army, a witness for the defence, being sworn, says:

Question by accused. You have said in your cross-examination by the accused, that while commanding in the city and harbor, New York, you understood that you had authority from Washington to consider all general hospitals under your command. Will you give the date and words of that authority, and say whether it did not relate solely to the exterior of the hospitals?

Answer. I referred to the hospitals in the city and harbor exclusively. The records of my office were turned over to my successor, and therefore I have not all the records of the case in my possession. I considered that I had control of all these hospitals. I have been recognized as such by the department at Washington, the Adjutant General's department, by the Surgeon General's department, and by the medical director and medical inspector of this city, as I understand.

On the application of the Surgeon General, I turned over Bedloe's island to the medical department for hospital purposes. I habitually visited the hospitals, and I discharged all men from the hospitals.

(The witness here submitted as a part of the answer to this question the papers appended, and marked M, N, O.)

I never considered it any part of my duty to interfere with what is called the interior management of the hospitals. I always abstained from all interference with the hospitals except in cases where my action was necessary. I never doubted my right to do so if I had been disposed. I was in the habit of inspecting the messes of the hospitals, both by myself and in company with the medical director, Surgeon McDougall. I considered that all the soldiers, all the sick, were under my command. All the sick that came into this city or harbor I considered to be under my command and my control. I gave them furloughs and gave them orders. Orders to them emanated from me, or went through me. I do not intend to be understood that that applies to any orders that the medical director or medical department may give to the sick.

Question by accused. You have said in your previous answer that while commanding the city and harbor of New York you never doubted your right to interfere with the internal management of the hospitals, if so disposed. Did you doubt your right to direct the treatment of the sick in hospitals, if so disposed?

Answer. I do not consider that I had any right to interfere with the prescriptions of the surgeons for the sick?

Question by accused. In your direct examination on the prosecution you alluded to referring the matter of Fitzsimmons back to the department headquarters. Did you mean the headquarters of General Canby or Major General Dix? Had the papers of Fitzsimmons, when presented to the accused, ever been at headquarters of General Dix?

Answer. The papers came to me from General Canby's headquarters, and I alluded to General Canby's headquarters in my answer. The remaining part of it I know nothing about.

In consequence of the illness of one of the members, a motion was made to adjourn until 10½ a. m. on Monday morning, which adjournment was ordered by a vote of the court.

R. T. FRANK,
Captain 8th Infantry, Judge Advocate.

GENERAL COURT-MARTIAL ROOMS,
New York City, December 21, 1863.

The court met pursuant to adjournment.

Present :

Major F. T. Dent, 4th United States infantry.
Captain William Clinton, 10th United States infantry.
Captain David P. Hancock, 7th United States infantry.
Captain Wright Rives, additional aide-de-camp.
Captain Thomas Lord, jr., aide-de-camp.
First Lieutenant Samuel T. Crowley, 4th United States infantry.
First Lieutenant Clarence M. Bailey, 6th United States infantry.
Captain Royal T. Frank, 8th United States infantry, judge advocate, and the accused also present.

The proceedings of yesterday having been read were approved by the court.

Hospital Steward John C. Moses, United States army, a witness for the defence, being duly sworn :

Question by accused. What is your position in the military service, and present duties ?

Answer. I am hospital steward in the regular army, and on duty as chief clerk in the McDougall general hospital.

Question by accused. Did you examine and direct copies to be made of an order by General Brown to the accused to arrest Private Fitzsimmons ?

Answer. I did.

Question by accused. Will you examine paper marked "B," in the record of this case, and say whether it is the order of General Brown referred to in your previous answer ?

Answer. I recognize it as the original order of General Brown.

Question by accused. What order immediately preceded the order of General Brown to the accused on the paper you saw ?

Answer. An order from General Canby to General Brown directing him to arrest Fitzsimmons and send him to Fort Columbus.

Question by accused. Please examine paper marked "A," in the record of this case, and say if it is the order of General Canby to General Brown to which you refer ?

Answer. I recognize it as the original paper.

Question by accused. What indorsement on the paper you saw immediately preceded the aforesaid order of General Canby to General Brown; will you produce a copy of the same ?

Answer. It was a reference of Provost Marshal General Fry to General Canby, commanding the United States forces in the city and harbor of New York. I here produce a true copy. It is appended, and marked "D."

Question by accused. What indorsement immediately preceded the reference of Colonel Fry, a copy of which you have just produced, and will you produce a copy of that indorsement ?

Answer. It was a communication from the colonel of the 40th New York volunteers, requesting Colonel Fry to have Fitzsimmons arrested and returned to his regiment. (A true copy of the communication is appended, and marked "Q.")

Question by accused. Were there any other indorsements on the application for the descriptive roll of Fitzsimmons?

Answer. There was not.

Question by accused. Was Private Fitzsimmons borne on the muster-roll of McDougall general hospital for October 31, 1863, forwarded to the Adjutant General?

Answer. He was.

Acting Assistant Surgeon P. C. Pease, United States army, a witness for the defence, being duly sworn:

Question by accused. What is your official position in the military service, and where were you on duty November 15, 1863?

Answer. I am the post surgeon at Fort Schuyler. I was on duty there November 15, 1863.

Question by accused. Did you accompany the officer of the day at Fort Schuyler on November 15, 1863, when he arrested Private Fitzsimmons, a patient in McDougall general hospital, and did you or the officer of the day see or examine the wound of Private Fitzsimmons previous to his removal from the McDougall hospital?

Answer. I accompanied the officer of the day, but neither of us made an examination of the wound.

Question by accused. Please state whether Fitzsimmons was not removed in a storm of rain from McDougall hospital and obliged to walk to Fort Schuyler?

Answer. It did rain at the time he was removed, and he walked to the fort.

Question by judge advocate. Did he walk with much or any difficulty?

Answer. I did not observe any difficulty in his walking; his wound was not of such a character as to affect his walking.

The accused having no more witnesses to introduce, asked to be allowed until 10½ a. m. on Wednesday to prepare his written defence, which was granted by the court.

The court then adjourned, to meet on Wednesday, the 23d instant, at 10½ a. m.

R. T. FRANK,
Captain 8th Infantry, Judge Advocate.

GENERAL COURT-MARTIAL ROOMS,
New York City, December 23, 1863.

The court met pursuant to adjournment.

Present:

Major F. T. Dent, 4th United States infantry.
Captain William Clinton, 10th United States infantry.
Captain David P. Hancock, 7th United States infantry.
Captain Wright Rives, additional aide-de-camp.
Captain Thomas Lord, jr., aide-de-camp.
First Lieutenant Samuel T. Crowley, 4th United States infantry.
First Lieutenant Clarence M. Bailey, 6th United States infantry.
Captain R. T. Frank, 8th United States infantry, judge advocate. The accused also present.

The proceedings of Monday having been read were approved by the court.

The accused then read and submitted his written defence to the court. It is appended to the proceedings.

The judge advocate asked to be allowed until to-morrow to prepare a reply, which was granted by the court.

The court then adjourned, to meet to-morrow at 10½ a. m.

R. T. FRANK,
Captain 8th Infantry, Judge Advocate.

GENERAL COURT-MARTIAL ROOMS,
New York City, December 24, 1863.

The court met pursuant to adjournment.

Present :

Major F. T. Dent, 4th United States infantry.
Captain William Clinton, 10th United States infantry.
Captain David P. Hancock, 7th United States infantry.
Captain Wright Rives, additional aide-de-camp.
Captain Thomas Lord, jr., aide-de-camp.
First Lieutenant Samuel T. Crowley, 4th United States infantry.
First Lieutenant Clarence M. Bailey, 6th United States infantry.
Captain Royal T. Frank, 8th United States infantry, judge advocate. The accused also present.

The proceedings of yesterday having been read were approved by the court.

The judge advocate here read his reply to the defence, which, together with the defence, is appended to the proceedings.

The court was then cleared, and after mature deliberation on the evidence adduced finds the accused, Assistant Surgeon Warren Webster, United States army, as follows :

Of the specification, first charge, guilty.
Of the first charge, guilty.
Of the specification, second charge, guilty.
Of the second charge, guilty.

And the court does therefore sentence him, Assistant Surgeon Warren Webster, United States army, to be confined to the limits of his post for six months, and to be reprimanded in general orders by the general commanding the department.

R. T. FRANK,
Captain 8th Infantry, Judge Advocate.
F. T. DENT,
Major 4th Infantry, President Court-Martial.

II. The major general commanding approves the proceedings of the court, as well as the sentence that Assistant Surgeon Warren Webster be reprimanded in general orders, and be confined to the limits of the post for six months. In consideration of his high standing, and his reputation for subordination anterior to the events which led to his trial, the court recommends the remission of the sentence. While acknowledging, as the major general cheerfully does, the professional merits of Assistant Surgeon Webster, he cannot permit so marked a breach of discipline as that which was clearly proved before the court to go unpunished. Believing, with the court, that the offence was founded in some degree on a misconception of duty, which, however, would have been more pardonable in an officer of less intelligence, the sentence of confinement to the limits of the post at which Assistant Surgeon Webster is employed is reduced from six months to sixty days.

JOHN A. DIX, *Major General.*

A.

HEADQUARTERS UNITED STATES TROOPS,
New York City Harbor, November 11, 1863.

Respectfully referred to Brigadier General Harvey Brown, who will have this man arrested and sent to Fort Columbus, thence to be forwarded to his regiment by first opportunity, accompanied with this paper.
By order of Brigadier General Canby.

C. T. CHRISTENSEN,
Assistant Adjutant General.

Received November 11, and referred to Assistant Surgeon Webster on the 12th.

H. B.

B.

HEADQUARTERS FORT SCHUYLER,
New York Harbor, November 12, 1863.

Respectfully referred to Assistant Surgeon Webster, United States army, in charge of McDougall hospital, who will comply with the above indorsement.
By order.

HARVEY BROWN,
Brevet Brigadier General.

Sent to Assistant Surgeon Webster on the day of date. Answer received from Doctor Webster on the 14th.

C.

McDOUGALL GENERAL HOSPITAL,
Fort Schuyler, New York, November 14, 1863.

Respectfully returned.
Conceiving that the general hospitals are under the sole direction of the Surgeon General of the army, I consider it my duty to obey orders directing the transfer of patients from this hospital only when received through the Surgeon General, or through his representative in this department, the medical director.
Respectfully submitted,

WARREN WEBSTER.
Assistant Surgeon United States Army, in charge.

D.

HEADQUARTERS FORT SCHUYLER,
November 15, 1863.

Captain Hannan, officer of the day, will, with a guard of six men, proceed to the hospital, arrest and bring to this fort Private Phillip Fitzsimmons, of company F, 48th regiment New York volunteers.
Captain Hannan will refer to Assistant Surgeon Webster, in charge of the hospital, and require him to send the man over to his charge. If Doctor Webster declines a report, the soldier will, if necessary, be forcibly brought. Cap-

tain Hannan will have no argument or controversy, or receive any papers or protest, but will simply obey these orders.

HARVEY BROWN,
Brevet Brigadier General.

Proceeded as directed on the within order. Saw Doctor Webster; made known the order, a copy of which was requested and given. On requesting information as to where the man could be found, was referred to the "hospital register;" on reference to which, ascertained the man was in ward 1, section B. Proceeded there with command. While there, medical officer of the day entered and asked if it was the intention to take the man away. On being answered "certainly it was," he left the room. Took the man from there without opposition, and delivered him in charge of the surgeon at the post hospital.

J. C. HANNAN,
Captain 28th Battery, officer of the day.

E.

HEADQUARTERS FORT SCHUYLER,
October 6, 1863.

Respectfully returned to Doctor Webster.

I have never taken, or had in my possession, any boat of the hospital department, nor did I, until I received a communication from Surgeon McDougall, know that the hospital department possessed a boat.

For the security of the post, and the prevention of desertions and the smuggling of liquor, I require (*vide* the accompanying copy of post orders) all boats to be kept at the wharf, and no boats to be landed elsewhere; and I presume that the boat alluded to by Doctor Webster is now at that place, and is exclusively subject to the orders of the medical department.

Doctor Webster has been furnished with all orders emanating from me that in any manner affect the hospital, so that he may give the medical directors all the information he may desire.

I have only to add that I shall not in any manner interfere with the internal relations of the hospital, but that the peninsula and the borders thereof are within my command, and that I shall exercise such control there as in my judgment the good of the service requires, and that orders issued by me in relation thereto must be obeyed, until countermanded by higher authority.

I see no reason why there should be any collision, nor why the most perfect harmony should not prevail between the post and the hospital, and I have no wish whatever to exercise any other control than is required of me; and if the same feeling exists in the medical department, no trouble will arise.

HARVEY BROWN,
Brevet Brigadier General.

A true copy:

WARREN WEBSTER,
Assistant Surgeon United States Army, in charge of Hospital.

[Indorsement on the above.]

"Copy of letter to Assistant Surgeon W. Webster, United States army, by Brevet Brigadier General H. Brown, commanding Fort Schuyler, respecting the hospital boat."

F.

General Orders, }
No. 36. }   WAR DEPARTMENT,
        Adjutant General's Office, Washington, April 7, 1862.

1. The general hospitals are under the direction of the Surgeon General. Orders not involving the expense of transportation may be given by him to transfer medical officers or hospital stewards from one general hospital to another as he may deem best for the service.

2. The chief medical officer, to whom the charge of all the general hospitals in a city may be intrusted, will cause certificates of disability to be made out for such men as, in his judgment, should be discharged. He will be responsible that the certificates are given for good cause, and that they are made in proper form, giving such medical description of the cases, with the degree of disability, as may enable the Pension Office to decide on any claim to pension which may be based upon them. The certificates of disability will be signed by the chief medical officer, and forwarded by him to the military commander in the city, who shall have authority to order the discharge and dispose of the case according to existing regulations.

3. The final statements, and all the discharge papers, will be made out under the supervision of the military commander, and signed by him. Where the men are provided with their descriptive rolls there will be no delay in discharging them after their certificates of disability are acted on. But if they have no descriptive rolls, application will be made to the company commander for the proper discharge papers, and the men may be maintained at the hospital a reasonable time while awaiting them, to avoid their being turned off without means of support. The discharge will, in all cases, bear the date when the papers are actually furnished the soldier. (See note.)

4. When a man is received in any hospital without his descriptive roll, the fact will be immediately reported by the medical officer in charge to the military commander, who will at once call on the company commander, in the name of the Secretary of War, promptly to furnish the military history of the man, and his clothing, money, and other accounts with the government.

5. When too long a delay would arise in discharging the man because of the remote station of his company, application will be made by the medical officer to the Adjutant General for such account of the man as his records will furnish. To this partial descriptive roll the medical officer will add the period for which pay is due the man since his entry into the hospital. The man will then be discharged, and receive the pay and travelling allowances thus shown to be due him, leaving the balance due him on account of clothing, retained pay, &c., for settlement in such manner as may hereafter be determined. (See notes.)

6. The military commander's duties, in reference to all troops and enlisted men who happen to come within the limits of his command, will be precisely those of a commanding officer of a military post.

7. It is made the duty of each military commander to correct, as far as may be in his power, the evils and irregularities arising from the peculiar state of the service at this time, by collecting stragglers and sending them forward to their proper stations, or discharging them on certificates of disability, if, on examination by the chief medical officer, they be found unfit for the service.

8. The military commander in each city will have control of such guards as may be furnished to preserve discipline and good order at the several military hospitals. He will advise the Adjutant General of the army what number of companies will be required for such guards. He will cause them to be properly posted, relieved, and instructed.

9. Whenever the chief medical officer shall report a number of patients as fit to join their regiments, the military commander will give the necessary orders to have them forwarded in good order and under suitable conduct.

10. The chief medical officer in each city is authorized to employ as cooks, nurses and attendants, any convalescent, wounded, or feeble men who can perform such duties, instead of giving them discharges.

11. All officers and enlisted men of volunteers who are on parole not to serve against the rebels, will be considered on leave of absence until notified of their exchange or discharge. They will immediately report their address to the governors of their States, who will be duly informed from this office as to their exchange or discharge.

12. The duties of military commander, as above defined, will devolve, in the District of Columbia, on the military governor; in the city of Baltimore, on the commander of the middle department; in the city of Philadelphia, on Lieutenant Colonel H. Brooks, 2d artillery, hereby assigned to that station; in the city of New York, and the military posts in that vicinity, on Brevet Brigadier General H. Brown, colonel 5th United States artillery.

By order of the Secretary of War.

L. THOMAS,
Adjutant General.

NOTE to Par. 3.—The first sentence of this paragraph is modified to read as follows:

"The final statements, and all the discharge papers, will be made out under the supervision of the military commander, and signed by him, when the soldier is not in a United States hospital, or under the charge of a United States surgeon. But if he is under a United States surgeon, or in a United States hospital, the surgeon will, in either case, make out and sign the discharge and final statements, after the military commander has indorsed the authority to discharge the soldier upon the usual discharge and certificates of disability."

ADJUTANT GENERAL'S OFFICE,
August 26, 1862.

NOTE to Par. 5.—"In cases where too long a delay would arise in discharging a man because of the remote station of his company," and when no descriptive list, or partial descriptive list, can be obtained from this office, the men referred to will be discharged under this order, and an order given them on the quartermaster's department for transportation to their homes. This order will be signed by the same officer who signs the discharge. The quartermaster's department will furnish transportation to such men upon the presentation of this order, requiring them also to show their discharge.

By order of Major General Halleck.

E. D. TOWNSEND,
Assistant Adjutant General.

NOTE 2d to Par. 5.—The sentence "To this partial descriptive roll the medical officer will add the period for which pay is due the man since his entry into the hospital," will be understood to give him pay on this final statement from the muster next preceding his entry into the hospital until the date of his discharge.

Official:

———— ————,
Assistant Adjutant General.

G.

General Orders, }   WAR D. PARTMENT, ADJUTANT GENERAL'S OFFICE,
No. 308.   *Washington, September 12, 1863.*

The Medical Inspector General has, under direction of the Surgeon General, the supervision of all that relates to the sanitary condition of the army, whether in transports, quarters, or camps; the hygiene, police, discipline, and efficiency of field and general hospitals, and the assignment of duties to medical inspectors.

Medical inspectors are charged with the duty of inspecting the sanitary condition of transports, quarters, and camps of field and general hospitals, and will report to the Medical Inspector General all circumstances relating to the sanitary condition and wants of troops and of hospitals, and to the skill, efficiency and conduct of the officers and attendants connected with the medical department. They are required to see that all regulations for protecting the health of troops, and for the careful treatment of and attendance upon the sick and wounded are duly observed.

They will carefully examine into the quantity, quality, and condition of medical and hospital supplies, the correctness of all medical, sanitary, statistical, military, and property records and accounts pertaining to the medical department, and the punctuality with which reports and returns, required by regulations, have been forwarded to the Surgeon General.

They will ascertain the amount of disease and mortality among the troops, inquire into the causes and the steps that may have been taken for its prevention or mitigation, indicating, verbally or in writing, to the medical officers such additional measures or precautions as may be requisite. When sanitary reforms, requiring the sanction and co-operation of military authority, are urgently demanded, they will report at once, in writing, to the officer commanding corps, department or division, the circumstances and necessities of the case, and the measures considered advisable for their relief, forwarding a duplicate of such reports to the Medical Inspector General.

They will instruct and direct the medical officers in charge as to the proper measures to be adopted for the correction of errors and abuses, and, in all cases of conflict of views, authority or instructions, with those of medical directors, will report the circumstances fully and promptly to the Medical Inspector General for the Surgeon General's orders.

Upon or near the beginning of each month medical inspectors will make minute and thorough inspections of hospitals, barracks, camps, transports, &c., &c., within the districts to which they are assigned, in conformity with these instructions, and the forms for inspection reports furnished them.

Monthly inspection reports, in addition to remarks under the several heads, will also convey the fullest information in regard to the medical and surgical treatment adopted; the advantages or disadvantages of location, construction, general arrangement, and administration of hospitals, camps, barracks; the necessity for improvement, alteration or repair, with such recommendations as will most certainly conduce to the health and comfort of the troops, and the proper care and treatment of the sick and wounded. When alterations, improvements, or repairs, requiring the action of heads of bureaus, are considered essential, special reports, accompanied by plans and approximate estimates of quantities or cost, will be made.

Medical inspectors will make themselves fully conversant with the regulations of the subsistence department in all that relates to issues to hospitals, whether general, field, division, or regimental, and will satisfy themselves, by rigid examination of accounts and expenditures, that the fund accruing from retained rations is judiciously applied and not diverted from its proper purposes, through the ignorance or inattention of medical officers, giving such information and instruction on this subject as may be required. They will also give close attention to the supervision of cooking by the medical officer, whose duty it is, under the act of Congress of March 3, 1863, and General Orders No. 247, of 1863, to "submit his suggestions for improving the cooking, in writing, to the commanding officer," and to accompany him in frequent inspections of the kitchens and messes.

They will exercise sound discrimination in reporting "an officer of the medical corps as disqualified, by age or otherwise, for promotion to a higher grade, or unfitted for the performance of his professional duties," and be prepared to submit evidence of its correctness to the medical board, by whom the charge will be investigated.

Medical inspectors are also charged with the duty of designating to the surgeon in charge of general hospitals and convalescent camps all soldiers who are in their opinion fit subjects for discharge on surgeon's certificate of disability or sufficiently recovered to be able for duty. In all such cases they will direct the surgeon to discharge from service, in accordance with existing orders and regulations, or return to duty those so designated.

Official communications to the Medical Inspector General will be directed to the Surgeon General, United States army, and plainly addressed on the left-hand lower corner of envelope, "for the Medical Inspector General," the name and title of the writer being written under the words "official business."

It is expected that all commanding officers will afford every facility to medical inspectors in the execution of their important duties, giving such orders as may be necessary to carry into effect their suggestions and recommendations; and it is enjoined upon all medical officers, and others connected with the medical department of the United States army, to yield prompt compliance with the instructions they may receive from medical inspectors on duty in the army department, or district in which they are serving, on all matters relating to the sanitary condition of the troops, and of the hygiene, police, discipline, and efficiency of hospitals.

By order of the Secretary of War.

E. D. TOWNSEND,
Assistant Adjutant General.

H.

MEDICAL DIRECTOR'S OFFICE, NEW YORK,
October 2, 1863.

Respectfully referred to the general commanding, with an earnest request that General Brown may be restrained from interference with the McDougall general hospital.

The ambulance referred to is for exclusive use for removal of sick and wounded.

The water for 1,500 patients, when nearly exhausted, should not be used for the animals of a neighboring post, nor should the hospital be the extreme resort in such cases. The hospital is not connected with the post, but self-sustaining. There is no necessity for clashing of interests, and it is much to be regretted.

C. McDOUGALL,
Medical Director, Department of the East.

Colonel D. T. VAN BUREN,
Assistant Adjutant General.

True copy:

WM. J. SLOAN,
Surgeon U. S. A

I.

OCTOBER 6, 1863.

The regulations and orders of the War Department place all general hospitals under the control of the medical department. Subordinate military commanders have no authority to interfere in their management.

H. W. HALLECK,
General-in-Chief.

True copy :

WM. J. SLOAN,
Surgeon U. S. A.

J.

SURGEON GENERAL'S OFFICE,
August 13, 1863.

*   *   *   *   *   *   *   *   *

The Surgeon General further directs that you inform Surgeon Phelps that the military commandant has no control in his hospital. The duties of military commanders, in connexion with inmates of general hospitals, are specifically defined in General Orders No. 36, of 1862, which same order declares general hospitals under the direction of the Surgeon General. In a recent case of interference with general hospitals, by Brigadier General B. S. Roberts, commanding district of Iowa, which was submitted to the Secretary of War, the Secretary decided in conformity with General Orders No. 36. The advice of Medical Inspector Lyman, as to compliance with the request of the military commandant, is deemed just and proper.

By order of the Surgeon General.

JOSEPH R. SMITH,
Surgeon U. S. A.

True copy :

WM. J. SLOAN,
Surgeon U. S. A.

K.

MEDICAL DIRECTOR'S OFFICE, D. E.,
New York, December 1, 1863.

The enclosed documents relative to a recent conflict of authority between Brigadier General Brown, U. S. A., and Assistant Surgeon W. Webster, U. S. A., general hospital, Fort Schuyler, are, at the request of the latter, respectfully referred to the general commanding the department, contrary to my suggestion, my own decision being on the main points adverse to the course of action of Doctor Webster, as will appear in the copy of my communication to him.

C. McDOUGALL,
Medical Director, Department of the East.

Received December 2, 1863.

L.

McDOUGALL GENERAL HOSPITAL,
Fort Schuyler, New York.

SIR : I have the honor to report that Philip Fitzsimmons, private of 40th New York volunteers, formerly of 38th New York volunteers, in ward one, section B, under my charge, is suffering from a gunshot wound of the left shoulder, which required a surgical operation for the removal of a portion of the clavicle on the 1st of November, 1863. The wound is now granulating favorably, but I do not consider him in a condition to be transferred from this hospital at present in any other condition than as a patient. His wound requires to be dressed twice a day.

I have also the honor to request that, in consequence of the critical condition of John Fallen, private of the 42d New York volunteers, company F, that all visitors may be excluded until I again report on his condition, and that no occurrence likely to occasion this patient any excitement may be permitted in this ward during this day. All of which is respectfully submitted.

JNO. J. CALDWELL,
Assistant Surgeon U. S. A., in charge of Ward.

WARREN WEBSTER,
Assistant Surgeon U. S. A., Surgeon in Charge.

M.

UNITED STATES MUSTERING OFFICE,
79 *White street, New York, April* 4, 1862.

GENERAL : The Herald's correspondent from Washington announced in the Sunday's issue that all volunteers arriving in this city, the sick, wounded, &c., would be taken charge of by the United States mustering officer. As no orders to that effect have been received, I presume it is a mistake. In view of this, however, I have communicated with the Bellevue hospital, and the authorities of that institution have agreed to receive the sick and wounded volunteers, who have no homes, and provide for them such accommodations as they have, and furnish them with the food and nursing of the hospital at the rate of ($3) three dollars per week per man. Two contracts are now in force with the New York hospital; the terms of one, exclusively New York volunteers, are ($50) fifty dollars per month, sick or no sick ; and ($4) four per week for each man. The bills under this contract are sent to this office for payment. Am I to continue to pay them? The terms of the other contract for all volunteers, excepting those from New York, are (75 cts.) seventy-five cents per day per man. Doctor Satterlee settles the accounts under this contract. I observe by this morning's paper that arrangements were made yesterday for converting a portion of the Park barracks into a hospital for the benefit of wounded soldiers arriving in this city from the seat of war. It is, in my opinion, a very unfit place for a hospital.

There should be some authority in this city designated, whose duty it shall be to attend to the returned volunteers. As matters now are, they are dependent upon the charity of the city. Under the present condition of things, I respectfully state that I am at a loss to know to what extent I am justified in disbursing on account of sick and wounded soldiers who belong to organized commands.

I am, general, very respectfully, your obedient servant,

W. A. NICHOLS,
Lieutenant Colonel U. S. Army, Mustering Officer.

The ADJUTANT GENERAL,
U. S. Army, Washington, D. C.

Indorsements.

Respectfully referred to the Surgeon General.
Park barracks should not be taken for hospital, as it is known to be unfit for that purpose.
By order:

> GEO. D. RUGGLES,
> *Assistant Adjutant General.*

ADJUTANT GENERAL'S OFFICE, *April* 8, 1862.

Respectfully referred to Brigadier General H. Brown, military governor, New York.

> GEO. D. RUGGLES,
> *Assistant Adjutant General.*

ADJUTANT GENERAL'S OFFICE, *April* 25, 1862.

> SURGEON GENERAL'S OFFICE,
> *April* 10, 1862.

Respectfully returned to the Adjutant General.
It would seem that the duties referred to by Lieutenant Colonel Nichols are devolved on Brigadier General H. Brown, by virtue of General Orders No. 38, (36) War Department, Adjutant General's office, April 7, 1862. The Park barracks have already been occupied as a surgical infirmary on proper authority. It is respectfully suggested that General Brown communicate with Surgeon Satterlee on the subject.

> R. C. WOOD,
> *Acting Surgeon General.*

N.

> ARMY MEDICAL PURVEYOR'S OFFICE,
> *New York City, April* 9, 1862.

GENERAL : I had the honor to submit to your consideration an official communication from the Acting Surgeon General, of date April 4, 1862, in relation to provision for sick soldiers arriving at New York, with instructions to confer with you and Colonel Tompkins on the subject. Surgeon McDougall having reported that you would assign the 12th infantry barracks, and hospital at Bedloe's island, for that purpose, on application by me, I have respectfully to request that orders may be given to that effect at your earliest convenience.

I am, sir, very respectfully, your obedient servant,

> R. S. SATTERLEE,
> *Surgeon U. S. Army.*

General HARVEY BROWN, U. S. A.,
Commanding Forts in N. Y. Harbor.

O.

> NEW YORK, *May* 28, 1862.

SIR : I have to request that you will apply to General Harvey Brown, commanding this station, for Bedloe's island and the buildings thereon, or, what would perhaps be preferable, for a building in Jersey City, to be used as a reception hospital for sick arriving in this city. It might be better to have both the above specified depots, one to be used for sick arriving by water, and the other for those arriving by land. The agents of the several States will, therefore, have nothing whatever to do with any sick soldiers but those turned over to them by the military authorities of this place—General Brown or yourself.

On receiving the buildings from the quartermaster's department, you will fit them up as hospitals, and for the present employ contract physicians to attend to them.

I am, sir, very respectfully, your obedient servant,

WILLIAM A. HAMMOND,
Surgeon General.

Surgeon R. S. SATTERLEE, U. S. A., *New York.*

Respectfully forwarded to General Brown. I am of opinion that, for the present, Bedloe's island will be sufficient if such arrangements are made as will insure the prompt transfer of such sick as may arrive at Jersey City, as well as those by land, to the island.

R. S. SATTERLEE,
Surgeon U. S. Army.

ARMY MEDICAL PURVEYOR'S OFFICE,
New York, May 28, 1862.

P.

WAR DEPARTMENT,
PROVOST MARSHAL GENERAL'S OFFICE,
Washington, D. C., November 10, 1863.

Respectfully referred to Brigadier General Canby, commanding United States forces, New York harbor, for his action.

By order of Colonel Fry.

WM. R. PEASE,
Captain U. S. A.

A true copy:

WARREN WEBSTER,
Assistant Surgeon U. S. A.

Q.

Copy of indorsement on Philip Fitzsimmons's D. L., " F" company, 40th regiment N. Y. volunteers.

Please have the within named soldier arrested and returned to his regiment. He was transferred from the 38th regiment N. Y. V. as absent without leave; since then we have received notice that he has deserted from hospital in Washington. He is now at Fort Schuyler, N. Y., and the surgeon sends daily almost for his descriptive list.

Very respectfully, your obedient servant,

T. W. EGAN,
Colonel 40*th N. Y. V.*

Col. J. B. FRY,
Pro. Mar. Gen., Washington, D. C.

A true copy:

WARREN WEBSTER,
Assistant Surgeon U. S. A.

DEFENCE.

The accused having been brought to trial upon the grave charges of "disobedience of orders" and of "conduct prejudicial to good order and military discipline," desires, before the court proceeds to deliberate and decide upon the question of guilt, to respectfully submit the following suggestions of defence:

It is confidently believed that, upon careful reading of the specification to the first charge, the court will find, in the first place, that the specification cannot, by reason of its want of distinctness and certainty, be made the basis of a verdict; and in the next place, that, if an offence by the accused is alleged therein with sufficient explicitness of fact and circumstance, there is not requisite evidence produced to sustain it.

The specification to the first charge nowhere alleges that General Canby addressed or directed any order to the accused. It nowhere sets forth that the accused received an order directed to him by General Canby.

So far as anything appears in the specification, the order of General Canby might have been directed to any one of a hundred persons, and none of them the accused.

It is respectfully submitted, that before the court can render a verdict of guilty on the first specification, it must find that the specification sets forth, in apt words, a lawful order; that such order was addressed to and read by the accused; and the order must be described with perfect precision, and not in vague terms.

The accused, therefore, humbly asks that the specification to the first charge be thrown out by the court, because it has no allegation of lawfulness, and has not that certainty, particularity and precision, which are required in specifications, by the custom and law of the service.

If, however, the court shall find the specification to the first charge sufficient in its averments, then the accused suggests that there has been no proof of any *order* from the Secretary of War, as the language of the specification would leave it to be inferred. There has not been and there is no documentary evidence that there has been an order from the War Department, or the Adjutant General, in respect to Fitzsimmons.

The statement of the specification and General Brown to the contrary is error.

The indorsement of Colonel Fry, of November 10, 1863, was but an indorsement of reference, and contains no word of command either to General Canby or Assistant Surgeon Webster, or anybody else. The Adjutant General of the army never, upon the evidence, saw or heard of it.

Again, there is utter absence of any proof that General Canby addressed an order to the accused, or that the accused received and read an order directed to him by General Canby.

There is evidence that General Canby addressed an order to General Brown, to have Fitzsimmons arrested, and the proof is conclusive that General Brown obeyed that order.

So that the only order in the case given by General Canby was obeyed.

As if to put it beyond all controversy that the order of General Canby was directed to General Brown, the last named officer swears distinctly, in his direct examination, that General Canby's order was directed to HIM. General Brown's language as a witness is as follows:

"On an envelope from department headquarters, New York city and harbor, was an *order* directing *me* to have the man arrested and sent to Fort Columbus."

Thus everything in the case—the papers, the official record, the testimony of General Brown himself—all unite to fix indubitably that the only order issued by General Canby was addressed to General Brown, commanding him, and not the accused.

There is testimony that General Brown gave Assistant Surgeon Webster an order, which was respectfully returned with reasons, but for that act of the accused there is no averment in the specification, and thus no charge. The concluding words of the first specification say, explicitly, that it was the order of General Canby which was disobeyed, and not the order of General Brown.

It is a familiar rule in courts-martial that a presumption of innocence attends the accused until it is overthrown by positive evidence; and applying that principle to the present case, if there be reasonable doubt in the mind of the court as to whether the order of General Canby was lawful, or can, in its legal effect, be fairly considered an order to Assistant Surgeon Webster, when it makes no allusion to him or the McDougall general hospital under his charge, then the accused is entitled to the benefit of the doubt, and for that reason, with the others assigned, there must be on the specification of the first charge a verdict of *not proven.*

And if the specification to the first charge be not proved directly against the accused, then, since (according to General Order No. 11, of February 5, 1862) a person can only be guilty of a charge by being guilty of the matter stated in the specification of the charge, there must be verdict of *not guilty* on the first charge in the present case.

If, however, the court shall be of opinion that the specification to the first charge is sufficient in its averments, and that all its material allegations are proven, then the accused humbly desires to be heard upon the larger question of disobedience of orders.

And, first of all, he prays that whatever he may suggest may not, under the circumstances, seem to any member of the court to be impertinent or unbecoming.

The accused does not fail to realize how humble is his rank in the military service ; beside that, he appreciates the fact that he belongs to a corps which, under existing regulations, cannot be represented in a court convened to try and, it may be, punish one of its members. And yet he feels that this is a court in whose presence and whose decrees an officer, even as humble as the accused, will have the same exact treatment and justice as would the highest officer in lineal rank in the army.

The accused recognizes to the fullest extent the vital necessity of military unity and subordination in order to secure the perfection of military operation.

He appreciates that in an army, or a department, there can be but one will, and that will supreme within its sphere. He knows that an officer is bound to obey the last order, not manifestly illegal, which is directed to him by the superior appointed over him, and leave consequences to take care of themselves. But none of those admitted axioms in military life, he submits with great deference, determine to which officers it is given by law to discharge or transfer patients from general hospitals.

It is important to bear in mind that nothing in the present case touches or questions the power or authority of Major General Dix, the department commander, to order a medical officer in charge of a general hospital to deliver up for transfer any patients under his charge. The accused never has hesitated to obey the orders of the department commander in respect to the management of the hospital, because, among other things, he considers himself bound to assume that every order issued from that source has the concurrence of his superior medical authority, which is the medical director on the staff of the department commander.

The order now in controversy, however, did not emanate from the Adjutant General of the army or Major General Dix, and the question now raised in respect to control of general hospitals is not an issue between the medical department and line officers, but is an inquiry whether the military commander in the city of New York, or the commander of the post at Fort Schuyler, can, like the department commander, exercise control over patients in general hospitals.

Neither is this a question of the authority of a post commander over his own post hospital and post surgeon, but, as just stated, it relates solely, in the opinion of the accused, to the amount of jurisdiction which subordinate military commanders have, independent of the department commander and the Surgeon General, over general hospitals.

The present case finds that Fitzsimmons was a deserter from the 40th regiment of New York volunteers; that he, in some way, found himself in general hospital on Governor's island; that on the 15th of October, 1863, he was, through Medical Director McDougall, transferred as a patient to McDougall general hospital; that, November 1, 1863, a severe surgical operation was performed on him; that eleven days thereafter General Brown ordered the accused to arrest the man and send him to Fort Columbus; that at that time the man was, by the surgical operation, confined to his ward, his wound dressed twice each day, and his arrest and transfer dangerous to his life; that the surgeon in charge of the ward reported him unable to be moved, except as a patient; that the accused indorsed on the back of General Brown's order the following:

"Conceiving that the general hospitals are under the sole direction of the Surgeon General of the army, I consider it my duty to obey orders directing the transfer of patients from this hospital only when received through the Surgeon General, or through his representative in this department, the medical director."

That General Brown thereupon directed his officer of the day to remove the man by force from the general hospital, which was done; that the man was taken out, without medical examination, by the persons removing him, into the place or condition of his wound, and in a cold rain-storm made to walk a long distance, and, in the end, sent to Fort Columbus, where it was found that he was not fit or able to be returned to his regiment.

The accused, it is alleged, offended by respectfully representing to General Brown the opinion of the accused that general hospitals are under the direction of the Surgeon General, and, therefore, that orders directing transfer of patients must come through that officer or his representative in the department, the medical director.

Is punishment to be inflicted for making such representation? Did not general orders, special orders, and the custom of the medical department, warrant such an interpretation?

General Orders Nos. 36, of 1862, and 308, of 1863, it will be remembered, start with the unconditional statement that general hospitals are under the direction of the Surgeon General. What can those orders mean if they do not bear out the construction given them by the accused?

The Surgeon General in an indorsement of August 13, 1863, directed to Medical Director McDougall, reiterates General Order No. 36, and says that the Secretary of War had decided, in a case coming up from Iowa, in conformity with this general order, and against the authority of Brigadier General Roberts, commanding the district of Iowa, to interfere with general hospitals. Not only that, but Major General Halleck, in an indorsement commenting on the conduct of General Brown in relation to McDougall hospital and produced here in court, maintained that military commanders, subordinate, like General Brown, to the department commander, had no authority to interfere in the management of general hospitals.

So, also, it has been proved here that Medical Director McDougall decided, in a case of conflict with General Brown, that the McDougall general hospital was self-sustaining, and not connected with the post at Fort Schuyler. How, if the court please, could a subordinate medical officer, like the accused, surrounded with such precedents and orders, but think an order like that of General Brown manifestly contrary to general orders and special decisions, and so unlawful? At least, will not this condition of rules and regulations prevent the court from finding that the accused acted either wilfully or with wrong intent?

The accused did not suppose that anything contained in General Order No 36, of April 7, 1862, in relation to the duties of the military commander in the city of New York, conflicted with this theory of the exclusive supremacy of the Surgeon General and the department commander in general hospitals. In the first place, General Order No. 36 must, he assumed, be so interpreted as to give force to all its requirements, and harmony of one part with another—that it must be read and construed as a whole. Its key-note and its starting-point are the declaration that "general hospitals are under the direction of the Surgeon General."

Then the second, third, fourth, and fifth clauses go on to provide, after again declaring that *all* general hospitals in the city are intrusted to the chief medical officer, how disabled men in hospitals are to be discharged from service by military commanders—not, as General Brown in his evidence would seem to intimate, upon his own will, but only on certificate of a medical officer. Then the sixth clause defines that "the military commander's duties, in reference to all troops and enlisted men who happen to come within the limits of his command, will be precisely those of a commanding officer of a military post." This sixth section harmonizes with the first section, by interpreting the words "all troops and enlisted men who happen to come within the limits of his command," to mean all troops and enlisted men except those in general hospitals, which, by a previous clause, are placed under sole charge of the Surgeon General.

So also the requirement in the seventh section, that military commanders collect "stragglers" and send them forward to their regiments, does not touch Fitzsimmons's case, for he was not a "straggler," the accused believed, within the meaning of General Order No. 36.

He was first a patient in the general hospital on Governor's island; was next regularly transferred by name to McDougall general hospital, by order of the medical director; was borne on the muster-roll of the latter hospital, and reported to the Adjutant General; and while in McDougall general hospital, was not only under its guards, but was enveloped by the sentinels of General Brown, who surrounded the peninsula on which that hospital stands.

The ninth clause of General Order No. 36 provides that the military commander cannot order patients in a general hospital to join their regiments, until the chief medical officer shall report them "fit."

The accused found in the clause of General Order No. 51, of May 10, 1862, which directs commanders of departments to designate some officer, *in each city or town where there is a general hospital,* to perform the functions assigned to military commanders in General Orders No. 36, what appeared to him a confirmation of the interpretation that the Surgeon General was to control the admission, management, treatment, and time of transfer and discharge of patients therefrom, and the military commander was only made responsible for their custody and transportation, when fit to be transferred, or for the authentication of their discharges when pronounced unfit for service by the medical officer.

And finally, as if to put to rest all doubt about the meaning of Order No. 36, the Secretary of War himself, in the Iowa case, had put upon it a construction which the accused assumed was conclusive everywhere, and which he ventures now to hold up as a shield against any threatened punishment.

In view of such orders and precedents, the accused implores the court to bear in mind that, even upon the testimony of the prosecution, this is not a case of disobedience of an order, where there was no reasonable ground to suppose the order was erroneously issued; and also to bear in mind what character for respectful, prompt obedience to superiors General Brown and Surgeons Abadie and Sloan—officers of long service in the regular army—give the accused.

General Brown testifies that he has "found the accused courteous and respectful," and "not captious or disposed to give annoyance." The testimony of Surgeon Abadie was to the same purport. There are no presumptions, then, that the accused intended or wished to give annoyance to General Brown in the present case. So far from that, the accused solemnly affirms that up to the occurrences now on trial, from no medical officer, in this department or elsewhere, did he ever hear the suggestion or intimation that the Surgeon General had not the entire charge of general hospitals. Medical officers with whom he has conversed, including those high and low in rank, have agreed in opinion that, according to the decisions of the War Department, no military officer in the department of the east, lower in command than Major General Dix, could, without intervention of the medical director, remove patients from general hospitals. The accused did not doubt that such was the law and rule of the service. He found in General Orders No. 65, of June 12, 1862, that "*each medical director* must, under the orders of his department commander, regulate the distribution of the sick and wounded to the hospital within the military department to which he belongs." This general order seems to make it clear, that no one but Major General Dix and Medical Director McDougall could regulate the distribution or transfer of patients. Again, in the same general order, the accused found provision that officers whose duty it is to forward detachments of men from hospitals, "will take care that no men except those provided with written passes from their hospital surgeon, or the medical director, shall be allowed to go."

So General Order No. 78, of July 14, 1862, appeared to the accused to confirm the constructions that a patient could not be ordered out of McDougall general hospital, without concurrence of the medical director, by an authority less than that of Major General Dix, whose order would be assumed to be by concurrence of the medical director, who is a member of his staff.

That order (No. 78) says that while in general hospital, "men will be under the fostering care of the government while unfit for duty; will be in position to be promptly discharged, if proper, and being always under military control, will be returned to their regiments *as soon as they are able to resume their duties.*" And by General Order No. 36, the chief medical director was the person to determine when men were "able to resume their duties."

In these allusions and comments on general orders, the accused has no wish to influence exposition or construction of existing orders in respect to general hospitals. He only desires humbly to lay before this court the reasons which constrained him to make the indorsement he did on General Brown's order, to the end that the court may not only judge of their correctness, but may consider whether or not the accused acted in good faith and as an honorable officer.

The act of Congress and General Orders No. 308, in evidence, recite that "the Medical Inspector General has, under direction of the Surgeon General, the supervision of ALL that relates to the sanitary condition of the army, whether in transports, quarters, or camps, the hygiene, police, discipline and efficiency of field and general hospitals; and the assignment of duties to medical inspectors."

"This General Order also directs surgeons in charge of general hospitals to yield *prompt compliance* with the instructions they may receive from medical inspectors on duty in the army, department, or district in which they are serving, on ALL matters relating to the sanitary condition of the troops and of the hygiene, police, discipline, and efficiency of hospitals."

Can it be denied that the propriety of removing from hospital a soldier with a wound as dangerous to life as that described by Surgeon Abadie, is "matter relating to the sanitary condition of troops" in hospital? And if not, then this order commands "prompt compliance with the instructions" in relation to such removal which surgeons in charge may receive from the medical department. Did Congress or general orders intend to place general hospitals under a double head of medical officers and officers not medical ?

It cannot be denied that the medical department, like every other staff department, must be and is secondary and subordinate to the line of the army, which does the fighting; but still that admission does not necessarily decide whether it has not been determined, by lawful authority, that the medical bureau shall have charge and control over men in general hospitals who cannot fight, and who are removed from the theatre of active operations in the field.

It appeared to the accused impossible that such general, all-embracing authority over general hospitals could be given to the medical department; that surgeons in charge of hospitals could be required to obey the Surgeon General . in respect to inmates, and yet that a subordinate commander in the line, with no claim to professional knowledge, had legal power to interfere and arrest the system which might be prescribed by competent medical authority. The court will recall the clear testimony of Surgeon Sloan on this point. It seemed certain to the accused that if General Brown had authority, independent of Major General Dix, or the medical director, to order one man out of the hospital, who was there as a patient, then he could order one hundred, and, in the end, could take away every male attendant and nurse, competent to administer to the wants of the suffering, and thus not only impair but *destroy* the efficiency and usefulness of the institution.

When the accused received the order of General Brown, unaccompanied by indorsement of Major General Dix, it was his purpose and intention to detain the man in his ward in custody, report his condition to the medical director and ask his direction.

His reply, when received, would have been scrupulously followed. If it be said that report of the condition of the man should have been made directly to General Brown, and not through the medical director, the accused replies, that upon such orders he has never made reports to General Brown, and never was instructed that it was his duty, or that it was regular to do so. General Brown states in his testimony, that—

" Dr. Webster makes no reports to me, and no reports of or from the hospital are made to the post." And he adds, " I do not conceive I have anything to do with the reception or dismissal of the patients or their treatment."

But the accused did respectfully inform General Brown that the man was a patient in the general hospital, and that, in the opinion of the former, the man should not be given up except on permission of the medical director.

The indorsement of the accused on General Brown's order covered both those points. And if it were not so, of what avail would have been any report to General Brown, who has testified that he considered his orders from General Canby " to be imperative," and thus to afford no opportunity for discretion? If discretion could be exercised in favor of a patient, it could have been on information that the man was a patient. But when General Brown gave the order to Captain Hannan to proceed with a guard of six soldiers and arrest the wounded man, there was no opportunity to state his condition, because the former directed the latter to receive no " papers or protest, but to simply obey the orders" to arrest and take away the man.

The accused solemnly reiterates that at the time he made the indorsement in question on the order of General Brown, he was inspired by no thought, purpose or wish but to obey implicitly the commands of the superiors set over him, in respect to the management of the general hospital placed in his charge. He was moved by no spirit of disrespect to General Brown. An order of arrest and transportation of a patient, unapproved by the medical director, had never before come under his observation, either in the McDougall hospital or in the Douglas hospital in Washington, of which latter institution the accused was for a long time in charge. His previous conviction of what the rules of the service required were strengthened on careful inspection of all the indorsements in the present case, by finding that the letters of Colonels Egan and Fry, and the order of General Canby to General Brown, assumed the man to be at the post of Fort Schuyler, and not in the general hospital. The experience of the accused had been, as Assistant Medical Director Sloan testified his own to be, that soldiers in the McDougall general hospital were *uniformly* described in orders and official papers as being in that hospital, and not merely at Fort Schuyler. If there was error of judgment and opinion in all this, it was an honest error, unaccompanied by any wilful or wrong intent. The accused believed that if Colonel Fry or General Canby had supposed the man to be in McDougall general hospital, they would have transmitted the recommendation or order, through the medical director, to the surgeon in charge, and not have issued the order to General Brown. He was convinced that if, with a patient having a wound as serious as what Surgeon Abadie and Doctor Caldwell have described Fitzsimmons's to be, he had, without a protest, permitted the arrest and transfer unbeknown to Major General Dix or the medical director, he would have received a rebuke, if nothing more, from his medical superiors.

In respect to the documents (marked M, N and O, respectively,) which General Brown volunteered to put in as testimony in the case, as if to make apparent the true legal relation existing in November last between the McDougall general hospital and the general commanding in the city and harbor of New York, the accused only desires to say that they have no possible bearing on the issues on trial. The first two (marked M and N) were written previous to the passage of the act of Congress of April 16, 1862, which effected such radical changes in the medical department, and are both prior to the issue of all general orders put in evidence here.

As to the remaining document, (marked O,) written one month after the passage of the aforementioned act, but ten days before the date of General Order No. 36, of April 7, 1862, it only directs conference with General Brown in respect to the appropriation of Bedloe's island and a place in New Jersey, by the medical department.

Thus much has the accused deemed it proper to say in exposition of the grounds of his action. It now remains with the court to find—

1. Whether the indorsement by the accused on the order of General Brown was a military offence.

2. If an offence, whether it has been set forth in proper military form in the specification to the first charge.

3. What punishment shall be inflicted if the first two points are found against the accused.

In regard to the last inquiry, the first two having been subjects of consideration, the accused, in mitigation of sentence, can only point to the record of his humble service, as it has been entered on the records of this trial. Others have succeeded better and done more, but none have tried harder to discharge all the obligations of duty. As post surgeon at Fort Larned in 1860; as assistant surgeon in charge of Douglas hospital in Washington; as medical inspector of the army of the Potomac, by order of the general commanding; as assistant surgeon in charge of the McDougall hospital, the accused has, under the orders of his superiors, striven to his utmost to promote the well-being of the sick and wounded, and the efficiency of the medical department. Errors of judgment on his part, there are doubtless many which he has committed; but errors of intention or wilful neglect, none.

To the specification in the second charge, the accused on arraignment, not wishing to even seem to deny the commission of any act done by him, pleaded guilty, although the inexactness of a portion of the specification, in respect to failing to give any assistance, is made apparent by the return of Captain Hannan. The accused, however, cannot deny that he forbade Captain Hannan to enter the wards of the hospital. He was inspired thereto in part by the reasons before assigned in his comments upon the first charge, but chiefly by the following report, already in evidence, and received from A. A Surgeon Caldwell, who was the medical officer immediately in charge of Fitzsimmons:

Ex. Doc. 21——3

Sir : I have the honor to report that Philip Fitzsimmons, private of 4th New York volunteers, formerly of 38th New York volunteers, in ward *one*, section B, under my charge, is suffering from a gun-shot wound of the left shoulder, which required a surgical operation for the removal of a portion of the clavicle on the 1st of November, 1863.

The wound is now granulating favorably, but I do not consider him in a condition to be transferred from this hospital at present in any other condition than as a patient. His wound requires to be dressed twice a day.

I have also the honor to request that, in consequence of the critical condition of John Fallon, private of the 42d New York volunteers, company F, all visitors may be excluded until I again report on his condition, and that no occurrence likely to occasion this patient any excitement may be permitted in this ward during this day.

All of which is respectfully submitted, by

JOHN J. CALDWELL,

A. A. Surgeon U. S. A., in charge of Wards 1 and 2, Section B

Warren Webster,

Assistant Surgeon U. S. A., Surgeon in charge.

The accused assumed that the hospital was, in circumstances like these, sufficiently under his charge to exclude any officer who, like Captain Hannan, was not of the medical department. He did not suppose it was prejudicial to good order and military discipline to thus comply with the request of the surgeon in charge of a patient in order to save life.

If the language of the accused would not be liable to misinterpretation, he could say that it is not he who, in respect to Fitzsimmons, has done acts " prejudicial to good order and military discipline."

The court cannot fail to remember the earnestness with which Surgeon Sloan, assistant medical director, condemned interference with general hospitals by subordinate commanders. He said : " It had been the source of a great deal of trouble and controversy. It has sometimes counteracted regulations adopted by the medical department. All the general hospitals in this department are governed by certain regulations and instructions. Interference with those regulations, without the knowledge of the medical director, has caused a great deal of trouble and annoyance."

How important it is to preserve rules and regulations unimpaired in the McDougall general hospital will be appreciated by perception of the fact that this institution has a capacity of two thousand beds, and a corresponding staff of assistant surgeons, hospital stewards, female nurses, and members of the Invalid corps. To regulate so large a command of sick and wounded, it is easy to see that system and subordination to one will are vital. The surgeon in charge is held responsible not only for the public property there in use, and for making the institution, so far as may be, pecuniarily self-sustaining, but for the good and judicious treatment of each one of the inmates. Is not everything which interrupts the regular order prescribed for such an hospital " prejudicial to good order and military discipline?" That the accused maintained good order and good treatment there is not denied; and he invokes to his aid the evidence of his character as an officer, given by those who testified to it, and to the condition and management of the hospital under his charge. If the record discloses to the court that the accused has been generally neglectful of his duties, unmindful of the sick and wounded intrusted to his care, or disrespectful in any sense to the superiors appointed over him, then let adverse judgment be pronounced. But if, on the contrary, he has earned a character as an officer worthy of approbation, then the accused asks that it may, so far as justice permits, enter into, and with the proof, in respect to general and special orders, ~~and~~ control the finding of this court.

WARREN WEBSTER,
Assistant Surgeon United States Army.

REPLY.

In reply to the able defence of Dr. Webster, which was read to the court yesterday, the judge advocate begs leave to state, first, that if there had been any objections to the specification under the first charge, for want of exactness in describing the offence, either in regard to the time, place, or nature of the offence, the proper time for making these objections was before he pleaded to them. Having pleaded to the charges and specification, and proceeded to the trial, if the offence has been proven, the court is bound to find a verdict of guilty, though it be proven to have been committed under circumstances different from those set forth in the specification, provided it comes within the jurisdiction of the court. It is not, therefore, essential that military charges should be drawn with the same precision and exactness as are indictments before civil courts. It is not believed, however, that the charges and specification now under consideration are open to any of these objections.

The accused alleges, that as the order of General Canby was not addressed to him, he could not be charged with disobeying it. The order reads: "Respectfully referred to Brigadier General Harvey Brown, who will *have* the man arrested," &c. This order, as well as the order from the War Department, (Provost Marshal General's office,) upon which the order of General Canby was based, was sent to Dr. Webster by General Brown, with directions from him. General Brown, in the following words: "Respectfully referred to Assistant Surgeon Webster, U. S. A., in charge of the McDougall hospital, who will comply with the above indorsement." Dr. Webster being in charge of the hospital, it will be apparent to the court that this was the natural and usual way of executing the order, if not, indeed, the only way which the dictates of military courtesy would admit. If these orders were not read by Dr. Webster, after having been thus referred, to whom must the fault be laid ?"

Paragraph one of General Order No. 36, of 1862, says: "The general hospitals are under the directions of the Surgeon General. Orders not involving expense of transportion may be given by him to transfer medical officers and hospital stewards from one general hospital to another, as he may deem best for the service." It would seem, therefore, that the authority of the Surgeon General, from this paragraph, is limited to cases not involving expense of transportation, &c. The remaining paragraphs of this order, some ten in all, go to point out and define to a certain extent the duties of military commanders in this connexion, showing that certain duties devolve upon them, and certain authority exercised, though, by a recent decision of the General-in-Chief, subordinate military commanders have no authority to interfere in the *management* of general hospitals. I would call the careful attention of the court to General Order No. 36.

The order upon which General Canby's order was based emanated from the War Department, from the Provost Marshal General's office. It is nowhere alleged in the specification that this was the direct order of the Secretary of War, or that it passed through the hands of the Adjutant General of the army, though the order is as imperative as if it had. Dr. Webster is in error in saying that there is no evidence to show that General Canby's order was received or read by him. General Brown in his testimony says, after enumerating the different papers which he had received in the case, among which were the orders of Provost Marshal General Fry and General Canby, "I sent all the papers to Dr.

Webster, with an order for him to carry the order of General Canby into execution." It also appears, from the testimony on the defence, that all the orders referred to in this case relative to Fitzsimmons were received at the office of Dr. Webster and copied by his chief clerk. It is not for representing to General Brown, as intimated by the accused, "that conceiving general hospitals to be under the sole control of the Surgeon General," &c., that he has been brought to trial, but for failing to comply with the orders he had received, and this representation is understood to be his reason for not complying with them. The accused asserts, that while he was unwilling to obey the order of General Brown, or General Canby, commanding the city and harbor of New York, he would obey an order emanating from Major General Dix, because he would understand it to have the sanction of the medical director, thus making the department commander subordinate to a member of his staff, the medical director.

Fully appreciating the doubt and uncertainty with which the accused was surrounded from the apparent conflict between the recent orders and decisions in regard to general hospitals, and the practice which has been maintained in this city and harbor, yet, is it not the duty of all officers to yield obedience to orders received from their superiors not manifestly wrong or illegal? and if so, was the order of General Canby, or Brown, a wrong or illegal order? Irregularity in the transmission of an order does not render it illegal.

It seems, from the testimony in the case, that authority to a certain extent has always been claimed and exercised by the general commanding the city and harbor of New York, and that General Brown, as commanding officer of Fort Schuyler, has exercised certain authority over the McDougall general hospital; that this hospital is within the precincts of his command; and as there can be but one commanding officer at a post, he has always exercised the command of a commanding officer over that hospital, with some allowances.

It may be a question, therefore, whether the recent decisions and orders in regard to general hospitals are applicable to those established within the precincts of a military post—as, for example, the one on Governor's island, or the McDougall general hospital at Fort Schuyler. This view of the subject, however, as well as that taken by the defence, seems to the judge advocate to be somewhat irrelevant, the question before the court being one purely of military discipline. All orders from a superior should be promptly and unhesitatingly obeyed, unless they are manifestly illegal, and then they are disobeyed at the peril of the officer disobeying them. An illegal order is one that would subject the officer obeying it to some punishment for his act; and as all courts-martial would be disposed to act with the utmost leniency toward one who was being tried for an offence committed in obedience to the orders of his superior officer, there would seem to be but little excuse for committing this grave military offence. In the present instance, instructions had been issued from the War Department (the Provost Marshal General's office) to General Canby, commanding the city and harbor of New York, to arrest and forward to his regiment Private Fitzsimmons, of the 40th New York volunteers, under charge of desertion. The man was within the precincts of General Canby's command, and by committing the crime of desertion had become amenable to the law; and by becoming a patient in the McDougall general hospital, under the most favorable consideration of the case, would by no means absolve him from the responsibility to the law.

Being a patient in the hospital, under the charge of Dr. Webster, if he had been in an unfit condition to be removed, it was the duty of Dr. Webster to so report him, and this report or remonstrance would have relieved Dr. Webster from all responsibility in the matter. It appears, from the evidence in the case, that Dr. Webster refused to make any report in regard to the physical condition of the man, and, therefore, all the testimony in regard to his physical condition must be considered in this connexion. It appears, also, that ample provision was made by Brigadier General Brown for the careful removal of the man.

Upon the fact that Dr. Webster refused to make any report in regard to the condition of Private Fitzsimmons is based the evidence of Captain Hannan, and the allegations of the second charge and specification. The accused can certainly claim no immunity on account of the physical condition of Fitzsimmons, as he positively refused to make any report or statement in regard to his condition. It must also be remembered that this refusal of the accused to comply with the orders he received was deliberate and studied; that he received these orders, and after careful consideration sent his refusal to comply with them. He was afterwards waited on by General Brown, with more consideration of leniency than any subordinate officer had a right to expect from a superior officer whose orders had been disobeyed, and admonished of the consequences of the course he was pursuing; yet he steadfastly adhered to his first determination. Being an officer of considerable experience in military matters, and having thus deliberately refused to yield obedience to the orders of his superior officer, it is but a reasonable presumption to suppose that he had carefully considered all the features of the case, and determined to disobey them, and abide the consequences. It should, also, be borne in mind that the general commanding the city and harbor of New York received his appointment and authority from the same source from which the Surgeon General receives his, and his orders therefore, within the limits of his command, are equally imperative. The judge advocate would call the careful attention of the court to the evidence in the case, which on the part of the prosecution is brief, both verbal and documentary, and pertinent to the matter contained in the charges and specification.

Considerable of the testimony on the part of the defence is a matter of opinion, and that portion referring to the physical condition of Fitzsimmons is entitled to but very little weight, as it was shown that the accused refused to make any report as to the physical condition of the man, though told, if he would do so, that the order in the case would be suspended.

The high toned character of Dr. Webster has been established by every witness, both for the prosecution and defence. His reputation, both professionally and as a gentleman and an officer, is one which we all might envy. His valuable services in the army, as a medical officer, entitle him to the gratitude of every true soldier. His heretofore subordinate and respectful disposition is also entitled to the consideration of the court. But the court must not forget that it is called upon to decide one of the most grave and serious offences known to military law.

In conclusion, the judge advocate would call the careful attention of the court to the whole testimony in the case; and as the most vital interests of the service, as well as those of a most efficient and valuable officer, are concerned in the decision of the matter now before the court, he would most respectfully remind them of the importance of discharging their duties without *partiality*, without *favor*, and without affection. The intercourse of the judge advocate with the accused throughout the whole trial has been of the most pleasing and satisfactory character, while it is believed that his demeanor before the court as an officer must have attracted the admiration of all its members.

Hoping that no unfair inference has been drawn, and with all the facts and circumstances of the case before the court, the judge advocate begs leave respectfully to submit it to its decision.

R. T. FRANK,
Captain 8th Infantry, Judge Advocate.

There being no further business before it, the court adjourned *sine die.*

F. T. DENT,
Major 4th Infantry, President Court-Martial.
R. T. FRANK,
Captain 8th Infantry, Judge Advocate.

The undersigned, members of the court, feel constrained to request the remission of the sentence pronounced by the court against Assistant Surgeon Warren Webster. The high standing of that officer in his profession, his reputation for subordination anterior to the events for which he has been tried, induce the court (who are well aware of the fact "that obedience to orders is the first duty of a soldier") to think that Assistant Surgeon Webster's conduct in this case was not engendered by a spirit of captiousness, but *esprit de corps*, which in this case was exercised from a mistaken conception of his position in the premises.

F. T. DENT,
Major, 4th Infantry.
WILLIAM CLINTON,
Captain, 10th Infantry.
D. P. HANCOCK,
Captain, 7th Infantry.
WRIGHT RIVES,
Captain and Additional A. D. C.
THOMAS LORD, JR.,
Captain and A. D. C.
SAMUEL T. CROWLEY,
1st Lieutenant, 4th Infantry.
C. M. BAILEY,
1st Lieutenant, 6th Infantry.

HEADQUARTERS DEPARTMENT OF THE EAST,
New York City, January 26, 1864.

SIR : By direction of the major general commanding, I have the honor to forward herewith proceedings of a general court-martial in the case of Assistant Surgeon Warren Webster, U. S. A., together with the general order promulgating the same.

I am, colonel, very respectfully, your obedient servant,

W. E. BLAKE,
Captain and A. D. C.

Colonel JOSEPH HOLT,
Judge Advocate General, U. S. A.

General Orders ⎞
No. 2. ⎠   HEADQUARTERS DEPARTMENT OF THE EAST,
New York City, January 14, 1864.

1. Before a general court-martial which convened at New York city, by virtue of Special Orders No. 118 from these headquarters, of December 7, 1863, and of which Major F. T. Dent, 4th U. S. infantry, is president, was arraigned and tried Assistant Surgeon Warren Webster, U. S. A., upon the following charges and specifications, viz:

CHARGE 1st.—"*Disobedience of orders.*"

Specification.—In this : that he, the said Warren Webster, assistant surgeon U. S. A., in charge of the McDougall general hospital, having received an order from Brigadier General Canby, commanding the city and harbor of New York, (through Brigadier General Brown, commanding Fort Schuyler,) based upon an order from the War Department, (which said order accompanied the order of Brigadier General Canby, and was read by Surgeon Webster,) to arrest and send to Fort Columbus Private *Philip Fitzsimmons*, of company "F," 40th regiment of New York volunteers, a deserter and an inmate of his hospital, did refuse to obey the said order. All this at or near Fort Schuyler, New York, between the 10th and 15th of November, 1863.

CHARGE 2d.—" *Conduct prejudicial to good order and military discipline.*"

Specification.—In this: that he, the said Warren Webster, assistant surgeon U. S. A., in charge of the McDougall general hospital, having refused to arrest and send to Fort Columbus Private Philip Fitzsimmons, of company "F," 40th New York volunteers, did then have presented to him by Captain Hannan an order from Brigadier General Brown, commanding Fort Schuyler, directing him, the said Captain Hannan, to repair to the McDougall general hospital and arrest Private *Philip Fitzsimmons*, of company "F," 40th New York volunteers, did forbid the said Captain Hannan to enter any ward of his hospital, and did also fail to give him any assistance in carrying out the orders of Brigadier General Brown. All this at or near Fort Schuyler, on or about the 15th November, 1863.

To which charges and specifications the accused pleaded as follows:
To the specification to the first charge, "not guilty."
To the first charge, "not guilty."
To the specification to the second charge, "guilty."
To the second charge, "not guilty."

FINDING.—The court having maturely considered the evidence adduced, find the accused, Assistant Surgeon Warren Webster, U. S. A., as follows:
Of the specification to the first charge, "guilty."
Of the first charge, "guilty."
Of the specification to the second charge, "guilty."
Of the second charge, "guilty."

SENTENCE.—And the court does therefore sentence him, Assistant Surgeon Warren Webster, U. S. A., "to be confined to the limits of his post for six months, and to be reprimanded in general orders by the general commanding the department."

2. The major general commanding approves the proceedings of the court, as well as the sentence, that Assistant Surgeon Warren Webster be reprimanded in general orders, and be confined to the limits of the post for six months. In consideration of his high standing and his reputation for subordination anterior to the events which led to his trial, the court recommends the remission of the sentence. While acknowledging, as the major general cheerfully does, the professional merits of Assistant Surgeon *Webster*, he cannot permit so marked a breach of discipline as that which was clearly proved before the court to go unpunished. Believing, with the court, that the offence was founded in some degree on a misconception of duty, which, however, would have been more pardonable in an officer of less intelligence, the sentence of confinement to the limits of the post at which Assistant Surgeon *Webster* is employed is reduced from six months to sixty days.

3. The general court-martial of which Major F. T. Dent, 4th U. S. infantry, is president, is dissolved.
By command of Major General Dix.

D. T. VAN BUREN,
Assistant Adjutant General.

Official:

W. E. BLAKE,
Aid-de-camp.

HEADQUARTERS OF THE ARMY,
Washington, February 23, 1864.

SIR : In compliance with your reference to these headquarters of the Senate resolution of February 9, 1864, calling for information in relation to the authority which subordinate military commanders have over general hospitals, &c., I have the honor to report as follows :

1. "What authority, if any, subordinate military commanders have, by existing regulations, independent of the medical department, over general hospitals."

General hospitals are established in cities, at military posts, and at convenient points, for the accommodation of patients too ill to be kept with their regiments consistently with their proper treatment. Soldiers of different regiments and different armies may be collected in the same general hospital.

The assignment of patients to general hospitals and their transfer from one to another are regulated by the Surgeon General. The medical treatment and nursing of patients, the internal police, responsibility for supplies, and hospital fund and furniture of the hospital, belong to the surgeon in charge. In so far as these are concerned, a military commander has no right to interfere in its management. Should he know, or have just reason to believe, there was mismanagement or malfeasance in these matters on the part of the surgeon, it would be his duty to report it to the proper authority, that an investigation may be had, but he would not be justified in directly interfering himself.

The guard stationed at a hospital, to prevent disorder and desertion among the patients and to enforce regulations, is under a military commander, and cannot lawfully be subject to the command of a surgeon when there is such a commander present. It is the duty of such military commander and of the surgeon harmoniously to co-operate in preserving good order among the patients in the hospital and out. Hence, in case of riot or disorder in the building, which cannot be quelled by interference of the medical officers, with their ward masters and attendants, the surgeon should call upon the military commander to apply the force under his command for its suppression; and the latter should confine his authority strictly to the accomplishment of that object, in which he would very properly arrest the parties to the violence, and restrain them under guard until they could be tried by orders from the department commander, unless the surgeon should consider their health, as patients, to be endangered by their removal from the hospital, in which case the commander would have no right to insist on taking them, but the surgeon would be responsible for their safekeeping.

Should a commissioned officer, while a patient in a hospital, be guilty of a breach of discipline, a medical officer would have no right to arrest him, but should report him to the military commander, with the charges against him.

Outside the hospital it is the military commander's duty to arrest and return to the hospital patients absent without a pass from the surgeon, as well as those who may be found by the guard conducting in a disorderly manner; and it would be proper for the military commander to arraign these, or other offenders, before a garrison court which he might assemble, on charges which he, or the surgeon, might see fit to prefer.

2. "What distinction, if any, there is in that respect [the authority of subordinate military commanders, independent of the medical department] between field or post hospitals and general hospitals."

Field or post hospitals are for the accommodation of men of a particular command, and not, like general hospitals, indifferently for men from any part of the army. They are appendages to a regiment, brigade, division, &c., or to a post, and, as such, are under the military control of the commander of the regiment, brigade, division, &c., or post. Interference in the medical treatment of patients in such hospitals would not be proper on the part of a military commander. In case of misconduct on the part of the surgeon in this respect, or of any maladministration of his office, he would be subject to arrest by his military commander. The transfer of patients from one to another of the hospitals, within an army or military department, would be regulated by the medical director of the said army or department, who, being a part of the general staff of the commander of the army or department, would give orders by *his* authority.

3. "Whether the interests of the service do not require that all orders relating to the management of general hospitals, the reception, treatment, and transfer of patients, should pass through the Surgeon General, or his immediate representative, the medical director?"

It is a military maxim that all officers shall obey the last order which they receive from a superior, provided it be *legal;* that is, not in violation of any law. The interests of the service do not require any general regulation which shall be in conflict with this maxim, because the responsibility attaching to an officer who gives a *legal* but unauthorized order is well understood among military men. In the case of Surgeon Webster, whose trial seems to have set on foot this inquiry, it was not necessary that the order to surrender a deserter in his custody should proceed through the Surgeon General; and the medical director of the department of the east would not have been the immediate representative of the Surgeon General in that case, but the representative of Major General Dix, the department commander. Had Surgeon Webster represented to the officer calling upon him for the deserter that he was a patient whose life or limb would be placed in jeopardy by moving him, the officer would not have been justified in executing the order, without having it repeated, after reporting the circumstances to the power from whom it emanated.

It is an established regulation that *in general* all orders relating to the internal management of general hospitals, the reception, treatment, and transfer of patients, shall pass through the Surgeon General; but no assumption can be based upon this regulation either that medical officers shall, therefore, under any circumstances, be absolutely independent of all other military control, or that they have the legal right of themselves to exercise a purely military command. To yield to such an assumption would be productive of highly mischievous results, and subversive of the principles of military discipline. This view is sustained by the terms of the act defining the rank of medical officers—section 8, act approved February 11, 1847:

"That the rank of the officers of the medical department of the army shall be arranged upon the same basis which at present determines the amount of their pay and emoluments : *Provided*, That the medical officers shall not, in virtue of such rank, be entitled to command in the line, or other staff departments of the army."

This view is also sustained by the usages of service, and by the orders, regulations, and instructions from the office of the Adjutant General of the army.

Very respectfully, your obedient servant,

H. W. HALLECK,
General-in-Chief.

Hon. E. M. STANTON,
Secretary of War.

No. 3.

General Orders, } WAR DEPARTMENT, ADJUTANT GENERAL'S OFFICE,
No. 4.   }   *Washington, February* 12, 1847.

I. The following act of Congress relating to the military establishment of the United States is published officially to the army :

"AN ACT to raise, for a limited time, an additional military force, and for other purposes.

"*Be it enacted by the Senate and House of Representatives of the United States of America in Congress assembled,* That in addition to the present military establishment of the United States, there shall be raised and organized, under the direction of the President, for and during the war with Mexico, one regiment of dragoons and nine regiments of infantry, each to be composed of the same number and rank of commissioned and non-commissioned officers, buglers, musicians, and privates, &c., as are provided for a regiment of dragoons and infantry respectively, under existing laws, and who shall receive the same pay, rations, and allowances, according to their respective grades, and be subject to the same regulations, and to the rules and articles of war : *Provided,* That it shall be lawful for the President of the United States alone to appoint such of the commissioned officers authorized by this act, below the grade of field officers, as may not be appointed during the present session : *Provided,* That one or more of the regiments of infantry authorized to be raised by this section may, at the decision of the President, be organized and equipped as voltigeurs, and as foot riflemen, and be provided with a rocket and mountain howitzer battery.

"SEC. 2. *And be it further enacted,* That, during the continuance of the war with Mexico, the term of enlistment of the men to be recruited for the regiments authorized by this act shall be during the war, unless sooner discharged.

"SEC. 3. *And be it further enacted,* That the President of the United States be, and he is hereby authorized, by and with the advice and consent of the Senate, to appoint one additional major to each of the regiments of dragoons, artillery, infantry, and riflemen, in the army of the United States, who shall be taken from the captains of the army.

"SEC. 4. *And be it further enacted,* That to each of the regiments of dragoons, artillery, infantry, and riflemen, there shall be allowed a regimental quartermaster, to be taken from the subalterns of the line, who shall be allowed ten dollars additional pay per month, and forage for two horses.

"SEC. 5. *And be it further enacted,* That the said officers, musicians, and privates, authorized by this act, shall immediately be discharged from the service of the United States at the close of the war with Mexico.

"SEC. 6. *And be it further enacted,* That it shall and may be lawful for the President of the United States, by and with the advice and consent of the Senate, to appoint one surgeon and two assistant surgeons to each regiment raised under this act.

"SEC. 7. *And be it further enacted,* That during the war with Mexico it shall be lawful for the officers composing the councils of administration of the several regiments constituting a brigade, either regular or volunteer, in the service of the United States, to employ some proper person to officiate as chaplain to such brigade, and the person so employed shall, upon the certificate of the commander of the brigade, receive for his services seven hundred and fifty dollars, one ration, and forage for one horse, per annum, provided that the chaplains now attached to the regular army, and stationed at different military posts, may, at the discretion of the Secretary of War, be required to repair to the army in Mexico whenever a majority of the men at the post where they are respectively stationed shall have left them for service in the field; and should any of said chaplains refuse or decline to do this, when ordered so to do by the Adjutant General, the office of such chaplain shall be deemed vacant, and the pay and emoluments thereof be stopped.

"Sec. 8. *And be it further enacted,* That the President be, and he is hereby authorized, by and with the advice and consent of the Senate, to appoint two additional surgeons and twelve additional assistant surgeons in the regular army of the United States, subject to the provisions of an act entitled 'An act to increase and regulate the pay of the surgeons and assistant surgeons of the army,' approved June 30, 1834; and that the officers whose appointment is authorized by this section shall receive the pay and allowances of officers of the same grades respectively; and that the rank of the officers of the medical department of the army shall be arranged upon the same basis which at present determines the amount of their pay and emoluments : *Provided,* That the medical officers shall not in virtue of such rank be entitled to command in the line or other staff departments of the army.

"Sec. 9. *And be it further enacted,* That each non-commissioned officer, musician, or private enlisted or to be enlisted in the regular army, or regularly mustered in any volunteer company, for a period of not less than twelve months, who has served or may serve during the present war with Mexico, and who shall receive an honorable discharge, or who shall have been killed or died of wounds received or sickness incurred in the course of such service, or who shall have been discharged before the expiration of his term of service in consequence of wounds received or sickness incurred in the course of such service, shall be entitled to receive a certificate or warrant from the War Department for the quantity of one hundred and sixty acres, and which may be located by the warrantee, or his heirs-at-law at any land office of the United States, in one body, and in conformity to the legal subdivisions of the public lands, upon any of the public lands in such district then subject to private entry; and upon the return of such certificate or warrant, with evidence of the location thereof having been legally made, to the General Land Office, a patent shall be issued therefor. That in the event of the death of any such non-commissioned officer, musician, or private during service, or after his discharge, and before the issuing of a certificate or warrant as aforesaid, the said certificate or warrant shall be issued in favor, and inure to the benefit, of his family or relatives, according to the following rules : first, to the widow and to his children; second, his father; third, his mother. And in the event of his children being minors, then the legally constituted guardian of such minor children shall, in conjunction with such of the children, if any, as may be of full age, upon being duly authorized by the orphans' or other court having probate jurisdiction, have power to sell and dispose of such certificate or warrant for the benefit of those interested. And all sales, mortgages, powers, or other instruments of writing, going to affect the title or claim to any such bounty right, made or executed prior to the issue of such warrant or certificate, shall be null and void to all intents and purposes whatsoever, nor shall such claim to bounty right be in anywise affected by, or charged with, or subject to, the payment of any debt or claim incurred by the soldier prior to the issuing of such certificate or warrant : *Provided,* That no land warrant issued under the provisions of this act shall be laid upon any lands of the United States to which there shall be a pre-emption right, or upon which there shall be an actual settlement and cultivation : *Provided, further,* That every such non-commissioned officer, musician, and private who may be entitled, under the provisions of this act, to receive a certificate or warrant for one hundred and sixty acres of land, shall be allowed the option to receive such certificate, or warrant, or a treasury scrip for one hundred dollars, and such scrip, whenever it is preferred, shall be issued by the Secretary of the Treasury to such person or persons as would be authorized to receive such certificates or warrants for lands ; said scrip to bear an interest of six per cent. per annum, payable semi-annually, redeemable at the pleasure of the government. And that each private, non-commissioned officer, and musician, who shall have been received into the service of the United States since the commencement of the war with Mexico, for less than twelve months, and shall have served for such term or until honorably discharged, shall be entitled to receive a warrant for forty acres of land, which may be subject to private entry, or twenty-five dollars in scrip if preferred ; and in the event of the death of such volunteer during his term of service, or after an honorable discharge, but before the passage of this act, then the warrant for such land, or scrip, shall issue to the wife, child, or children, if there be any; and if none, then to the father; and if there be no father, then to the mother of such deceased volunteer : *Provided*, That nothing contained in this section shall be construed to give bounty land to such volunteers as were accepted into service, and discharged without being marched to the seat of war.

"Sec. 10. *And be it further enacted*, That it shall and may be lawful for the President, by and with the advice and consent of the Senate, to appoint from the officers of the army four quartermasters of the rank of major, and ten assistant quartermasters with the rank of captain."

"*Approved February* 11, 1847."

II. By the 9th section of the act, each non commissioned officer, musician, or private now in the service, or who may hereafter be enlisted during the present war with Mexico, and who shall receive an honorable discharge either by expiration of his term of enlistment, or for disability incurred in the course of his service, will be entitled to a warrant for *one hundred and sixty acres of land*, which he will be at liberty to locate in one body, upon any of the public lands that may be subject to private entry; or he may, at his option, when honorably discharged, receive *treasury scrip to the amount of one hundred dollars*, bearing six per cent. interest, payable semi-annually, and redeemable at the pleasure of the governments.

Officers will insert the provisions of this paragraph in their recruiting advertisement.

III. Under the decision of the Attorney General the *three months' extra pay* provided for cases of re-enlistment by the 29th section of the act of July 5, 1838, is only allowed to the soldier who "may re-enlist into his company or regiment," &c., for the period of *five years;* and if he re-enter the army for the term of "during the war" with Mexico, he will be entitled only to the twelve dollars bounty, under the second section of the act approved January 12, 1847.

IV. Each colonel, or other *permanent* commander of a regiment will appoint the regimental quartermaster, (subject to the approval of the Secretary of War,) and report the same to the Adjutant General. The appointments will be announced in regimental orders, and will not be vacated except by sentence of a general court-martial, or by the authority of the *permanent* commander of the regiment. These appointments will only be conferred upon subalterns, who, to experience in service unite high qualifications and sound practical discretion necessary for the efficient performance of the responsible and varied military duties of the station.

The regimental quartermaster will perform the functions of assistant commissary of subsistence, in addition to his duties as quartermaster of the regiment or post, if the command be less than a regiment.

By order.

R. JONES,
Adjutant General.

General Orders, } WAR DEPARTMENT, ADJUTANT GENERAL'S OFFICE,
    No. 43. }   *Washington, April* 19, 1862.

The following act of Congress is published for the information of all concerned:

AN ACT to reorganize and increase the efficiency of the medical department of the army.

Be it enacted by the Senate and House of Representatives of the United States of America in Congress assembled, That there shall be added to the present medical corps of the army ten surgeons and ten assistant surgeons, to be promoted and appointed under existing laws; twenty medical cadets, and as many hospital stewards as the surgeon general may consider necessary for the public service, and that their pay and that of all hospital stewards in the volunteer as well as in the regular service shall be thirty dollars per month, to be computed from the passage of this act. And all medical cadets in the service shall, in addition to their pay, receive one ration per day, either in kind or commutation.

SEC. 2. *And be it further enacted,* That the Surgeon General to be appointed under this act shall have the rank, pay, and emoluments of a brigadier general. There shall be one Assistant Surgeon General and one Medical Inspector General of hospitals, each with the rank, pay, and emoluments of a colonel of cavalry, and the Medical Inspector General shall have, under the direction of the Surgeon General, the supervision of all that relates to the sanitary condition of the army, whether in transports, quarters, or camps, and of the hygiene, police, discipline, and efficiency of field and general hospitals, under such regulations as may hereafter be established.

SEC. 3. *And be it further enacted,* That there shall be eight medical inspectors, with the rank, pay, and emoluments each of a lieutenant colonel of cavalry, and who shall be charged with the duty of inspecting the sanitary condition of transports, quarters, and camps, of field and general hospitals, and who shall report to the Medical Inspector General, under such regulations as may hereafter established, all circumstances relating to the sanitary condition and wants of troops and of hospitals, and to the skill, efficiency, and good conduct of the officers and attendants connected with the medical department.

SEC. 4. *And be it further enacted,* That the Surgeon General, the Assistant Surgeon General, Medical Inspector General, and medical inspectors, shall, immediately after the passage of this act, be appointed by the President, by and with the advice and consent of the Senate, by selection from the medical corps of the army, or from the surgeons in the volunteer service, without regard to their rank when so selected, but with sole regard to qualifications.

SEC. 5. *And be it further enacted,* That medical purveyors shall be charged, under the direction of the Surgeon General, with the selection and purchase of all medical supplies, including new standard preparations, and of all books, instruments, hospital stores, furniture, and other articles required for the sick and wounded of the army. In all cases of emergency they may provide such additional accommodations for the sick and wounded of the army, and may transport such medical supplies as circumstances may render necessary, under such regulations as may hereafter be established, and shall make prompt and immediate issues upon all special requisitions made upon them under such circumstances by medical officers; and the special requisitions shall consist simply of a list of the articles required, the qualities required, dated, and signed by the medical officers requiring them.

SEC. 6. *And be it further enacted,* That whenever the inspector general, or any one of the medical inspectors, shall report an officer of the medical corps as disqualified, by age or otherwise, for promotion to a higher grade, or unfitted for the performance of his professional duties, he shall be reported by the

Surgeon General, for examination, to a medical board, as provided by the seventeenth section of the act approved August third, eighteen hundred and sixty-one.

SEC. 7. *And be it further enacted,* That the provisions of this act shall continue and be in force during the existence of the present rebellion, and no longer : *Provided, however,* That, when this act shall expire, all officers who shall have been promoted from the medical staff of the army under this act shall retain their respective rank in the army, with such promotion as they would have been entitled to.

Approved April 16, 1862.

By order of the Secretary of War.

L. THOMAS,
Adjutant General.

Official :

————— ————,

Assistant Adjutant General.

———

General Orders, ⎱   WAR DEPARTMENT, ADJUTANT GENERAL'S OFFICE,
    No. 53.   ⎰   *Washington, May 16, 1862.*

The following acts of Congress are published for the information of all concerned :

I. AN ACT to provide for the deficiency in the appropriation for the pay of the two and three years' volunteers, and the officers and men actually employed in the western department.

Be it enacted by the Senate and House of Representatives of the United States of America in Congress assembled, That there be, and hereby is, appropriated, out of any money in the treasury not otherwise appropriated, the sum of thirty millions of dollars, or so much thereof as may be necessary, to enable the government to pay the two and three years' volunteers called into the service of the United States, being an additional amount required for the fiscal year ending June thirtieth, eighteen hundred and sixty-two.

SEC. 2. *And be it further enacted,* That there be, and hereby is, appropriated, out of any money in the treasury not otherwise appropriated, the sum of one hundred thousand dollars, or so much thereof as may be necessary, to carry into effect the act approved March twenty-fifth, eighteen hundred and sixty-two, to secure pay, bounty, and pensions to officers and men actually employed in the western department, or department of Missouri.

Approved May 14, 1862.

II. AN ACT to facilitate the discharge of enlisted men for physical disability.

Be it enacted by the Senate and House of Representatives of the United States of America in Congress assembled, That the Medical Inspector General, or any medical inspector, is hereby authorized and empowered to discharge from the service of the United States any soldier or enlisted man, with the consent of such soldier or enlisted man, in the permanent hospitals, laboring under any physical disability which makes it disadvantageous to the service that he be retained therein, and the certificate in writing of such inspector general or medical inspector, setting forth the existence and nature of such physical disability, shall be sufficient evidence of such discharge : *Provided, however,* That every such certificate shall appear on its face to have been founded on personal inspection of the soldier so discharged, and shall specifically describe the nature and origin of such disability ; and that such discharge shall be without prejudice to the right of such soldier or enlisted man to the pay due him at the date thereof, and report the same to the Adjutant General and the Surgeon General.

Approved May 14, 1862.

By order of the Secretary of War.

L. THOMAS,
Adjutant General.

Official :

———— ————,
Assistant Adjutant General.

————————

No. 4.

General Orders, }   WAR DEPARTMENT, ADJUTANT GENERAL'S OFFICE,
No. 36.   }   *Washington, April* 7, 1862.

1. The general hospitals are under the direction of the Surgeon General. Orders not involving expense of transportation may be given by him to transfer medical officers or hospital stewards from one general hospital to another, as he may deem best for the service.

2. The chief medical officer, to whom the charge of all the general hospitals in a city may be intrusted, will cause certificates of disability to be made out for such men as, in his judgment, should be discharged. He will be responsible that the certificates are given for good cause, and that they are made in proper form, giving such medical description of the cases, with the degree of disability, as may enable the Pension Office to decide on any claim to pension which may be based upon them. The certificates of disability will be signed by the chief medical officer, and forwarded by him to the military commander in the city, who shall have authority to order the discharge and dispose of the case according to existing regulations.

3. The final statements, and all the discharge papers, will be made out under the supervision of the military commander, and signed by him. Where the men are provided with their descriptive rolls, there will be no delay in discharging them after their certificates of disability are acted on. But if they have no descriptive rolls, application will be made to the company commander for the proper discharge papers, and the men may be maintained at the hospital a reasonable time while awaiting them, to avoid their being turned off without means of support. The discharge will, in all cases, bear the date when the papers are actually furnished the soldier. (See note.)

4. When a man is received in any hospital without his descriptive roll, the fact will be immediately reported by the medical officer in charge to the military commander, who will at once call on the company commander, in the name of the Secretary of War, promptly to furnish the military history of the man, and his clothing, money, and other accounts with the government.

5. When too long a delay would arise in discharging the man because of the remote station of his company, application will be made by the medical officer to the Adjutant General for such account of the man as his records will furnish. To this partial descriptive roll the medical officer will add the period for which pay is due the man since his entry into the hospital. The man will then be discharged, and receive the pay and travelling allowances thus shown to be due him, leaving the balance due him on account of clothing, retained pay, &c., for settlement in such manner as may hereafter be determined. (See notes.)

6. The military commander's duties, in reference to all troops and enlisted men who happen to come within the limits of his command, will be precisely those of a commanding officer of a military post.

7. It is made the duty of each military commander to correct, as far as may be in his power, the evils and irregularities arising from the peculiar state of the service at this time, by collecting stragglers and sending them forward to their proper stations, or discharging them on certificates of disability, if, on examination by the chief medical officer, they be found unfit for the service.

8. The military commander in each city will have control of such guards as may be furnished to preserve discipline and good order at the several military hospitals. He will advise the Adjutant General of the army what number of companies will be required for such guards. He will cause them to be properly posted, relieved, and instructed.

9. Whenever the chief medical officer shall report a number of patients as fit to join their regiments, the military commander will give the necessary orders to have them forwarded in good order and under suitable conduct.

10. The chief medical officer in each city is authorized to employ as cooks, nurses, and attendants, any convalescent, wounded, or feeble men, who can perform such duties, instead of giving them discharges.

11. All officers and enlisted men of volunteers who are on parole not to serve against the rebels will be considered on leave of absence, until notified of their exchange or discharge. They will immediately report their address to the governors of their States, who will be duly informed from this office as to their exchange or discharge.

12. The duties of military commanders, as above defined, will devolve, in the District of Columbia, on the military governor; in the city of Baltimore, on the commander of the middle department; in the city of Philadelphia, on Lieutenant Colonel H. Brooks, 2d artillery, hereby assigned to that station; in the city of New York, and the military posts in that vicinity, on Brevet Brigadier General H. Brown, colonel 5th United States artillery.

By order of the Secretary of War:

L. THOMAS,
Adjutant General.

NOTE to Par. 3.—The first sentence of this paragraph is modified to read as follows :

The final statements, and all the discharge papers, will be made out under the supervision of the military commander, and signed by him, when the soldier is not in a United States hospital, or under the charge of a United States surgeon. But if he is under a United States surgeon or in a United States hospital, the surgeon will, in either case, make out and sign the discharge and final statements, after the military commander has indorsed the authority to discharge the soldier upon the usual discharge and certificates of disability.

ADJUTANT GENERAL'S OFFICE,
August 26, 1862.

NOTE to Par. 5.—"In cases where too long a delay would arise in discharging a man because of the remote station of his company," and when no descriptive list or partial descriptive list can be obtained from this office, the men referred to will be discharged under this order, and an order given them on the quartermaster's department for transportation to their homes. This order will be signed by the same officer who signed the discharge. The quartermaster's department will furnish transportation to such men, upon the presentation of this order, requiring them also to show their discharge.

By order of Major General Halleck.

E. D. TOWNSEND,
Assistant Adjutant General.

NOTE 2d to Par. 5.—The sentence "to this partial descriptive roll to the medical officer will add the period for which pay is due the man since his entry into the hospital," will be understood to give him pay *on this final statement* from the muster *next preceding* his entry into the hospital until the date of his discharge.

Official:

———— ————,

Assistant Adjutant General.

General Orders, }   WAR DEPARTMENT, ADJUTANT GENERAL'S OFFICE,
No. 65. }   *Washington, June* 12, 1862.

I. Paragraph 1269 army regulations is hereby so modified that private physicians, employed as medical officers with an army in the field in time of war, may be allowed a sum not to exceed one hundred and twenty-five dollars per month, besides transportation in kind.

II. The certificates of discharge to be given by the Medical Inspector General, or any medical inspector of the army, under the act of May 14, 1862, published in "General Orders" No. 53, will be made on the printed forms for certificates of disability prescribed by the army regulations. The inspector giving the discharge will indorse it with his own certificate, that it is granted upon his own personal inspection of the soldier, and with the soldier's consent; and for disability, the nature, degree, and origin of which are correctly described in the within certificate.

III. Each medical director must, under the orders of his department commander, regulate the distribution of the sick and wounded to the hospitals within the military department to which he belongs. When want of room in such hospitals, or the nature of the wounds or diseases of any invalids, require that detachments shall be sent beyond the limits of their departments, the Surgeon General will designate to the medical directors, either by general instructions, or specially by telegraph, to what points they shall be sent. Officers, whose duty it may become to forward such detachments, will take care that no men, except those provided with written passes from their hospital surgeon or the medical director, shall be allowed to go.

Furloughs will not be given by captains of companies or colonels of regiments on any pretext whatever. A furlough from such authority will not relieve a soldier from the charge of desertion.

Enlisted men absent from their regiments without proper authority, are in fact *deserters*, and not only forfeit all pay and allowances, but are subject to the penalties awarded by law to such offenders. No plea of sickness, or other cause not *officially* established, and no certificate of a physician in civil life, unless it be approved by some officer acting as a military commander, *will hereafter avail to remove the charge of desertion, or procure arrears of pay*, when a soldier has been mustered as absent from his regiment *without leave.*

By application to the governors of their States, or to any military commander or United States mustering officer in a city, transportation can be procured to their regiments by soldiers who are otherwise unable to join them.

Where no military commander has been appointed, the senior officer of the army on duty as mustering or recruiting officer in the place, is hereby authorized and required to act in that capacity until another may be appointed.

Under "General Orders" No. 36, it is the duty of military commanders to collect all stragglers and forward them to their regiments. To do this, they must establish camps or depots, under strict military discipline, and maintain sufficient guards to enforce this order. Convalescents in army hospitals will be reported by the surgeons in charge to the military commanders, to be kept at their camps or depots until they can be sent to join their regiments. Muster-rolls of each detachment will be made out from the best data at hand, the statement of the men being taken in the absence of other information concerning them. A duplicate of each muster-roll must be forwarded to the Adjutant General the day the detachment starts.

To avoid confusion and retain necessary control over all soldiers in the United States service, those who are entertained in State or private hospitals must be subject to the nearest military commander, and are hereby required to report to him in person as soon as they become convalescent.

Immediately after receipt of this order, each military commander will publish, three times, in some newspaper, a brief notice requiring all United States soldiers in that city and country around, who are not under treatment in a United States hospital, to report themselves to him without delay, on penalty of being considered deserters. In cases of serious disability from wounds or sickness, which may prevent obedience to this requirement, the soldier must furnish a certificate of a physician of good standing, describing his case, on which, if satisfactory, the military commander may grant a written furlough for not exceeding thirty days, or a discharge on the prescribed form of a certificate of disability, made out strictly according to the regulations. But no discharges will be given on account of rheumatism, or where there is a prospect of recovery within a reasonable time.

Military commanders may discharge men *at their own request*, who exhibit to them satisfactory proof of their being *paroled* prisoners of war. To other paroled men they will give furloughs until notified of their exchange, or discharged from the service.

Military commanders will report to the Adjutant General, tri-monthly, the names, companies, regiments, and residences of all the soldiers furloughed or discharged by them; and forward, at the same time, the certificates of disability in case of discharge.

They will make timely requisitions for the blanks, and such other things as may be necessary for the proper execution of this order.

By order of the Secretary of War:

L. THOMAS, Adjutant General.

Official:

———— ————,
Assistant Adjutant General.

General Orders, }   WAR DEPARTMENT, ADJUTANT GENERAL'S OFFICE,
    No. 78. }   *Washington, July* 14, 1862.

I. The many evils which arise from giving furloughs to enlisted men require that the practice shall be discontinued. Hospitals, provided with ample medical attendance, nurses, food, and clothing, are established by the government, at great expense, not only near the scenes of active military operations, but in many of the northern States. When it is expedient and advisable, sick and wounded patients may, under the direction of the Surgeon General, be transferred in parties, but not in individual cases, to hospitals at the north; and, as far as practicable, the men will be sent to States in which their regiments were raised, provided United States hospitals have been established there. Such regulations will be adopted at all the hospitals as will permit relatives and friends to visit the patients, and furnish them with comforts, at such hours and in such manner as will not interfere with the discipline of the hospitals and the welfare of the mass of patients. The men will thus be under the fostering care of the government while unfit for duty; will be in position to be promptly discharged if proper, and, being always under military control, will be returned to their regiments as soon as they are able to resume their duties. The unauthorized removal of soldiers from under the control of the United States authorities, by any agents whatever, subjects them to loss of pay and other penalties of desertion.

II. At large camps, depots, or posts, where absentees arrive *en route* to their companies, the commanding officer will immediately set apart a particular place where the men may be quartered, in buildings, tents, or huts, as soon as they arrive, and may, *without delay*, receive food and clothing. Parties will be detailed to await at landing places the arrival of such soldiers, and to direct them to their quarters. They will be assigned immediately to temporary companies, composed as far as possible of men from the same regiments or brigades; and each of these companies will be forwarded in a body to the command to which they belong, according to the directions contained in paragraph I of "General Orders" No. 72.

III. Chaplains appointed by the President for hospitals will be assigned by the Surgeon General to hospitals in the cities for which they were appointed. Should the breaking up of a hospital leave a chaplain supernumerary in any city, the fact will be immediately reported to the Adjutant General. Chaplains will be subordinate to the hospital surgeons. Leaves of absence will be granted them by the Surgeon General when approved by the surgeons in charge of their hospitals.

By order of the Secretary of War.

L. THOMAS,
Adjutant General.

Official:

———— ————,
Assistant Adjutant General.

————

General Orders, }   WAR DEPARTMENT, ADJUTANT GENERAL'S OFFICE,
No. 308. }   *Washington, September 12, 1863.*

The Medical Inspector General has, under direction of the Surgeon General, the supervision of all that relates to the sanitary condition of the army, whether in transports, quarters, or camps; the hygiene, police, discipline, and efficiency of field and general hospitals; and the assignment of duties to medical inspectors.

Medical inspectors are charged with the duty of inspecting the sanitary condition of transports, quarters, and camps of field and general hospitals, and will report to the Medical Inspector General all circumstances relating to the sanitary condition and wants of troops and of hospitals, and to the skill, efficiency, and conduct of the officers and attendants connected with the medical department. They are required to see that all regulations for protecting the health of troops, and for the careful treatment of and attendance upon the sick and wounded, are duly observed.

They will carefully examine into the quantity, quality, and condition of medical and hospital supplies, the correctness of all medical, sanitary, statistical, military, and property records and accounts pertaining to the medical department, and the punctuality with which reports and returns, required by regulations, have been forwarded to the Surgeon General.

They will ascertain the amount of disease and mortality among the troops, inquire into the causes, and the steps that may have been taken for its prevention or mitigation, indicating, verbally or in writing, to the medical officers, such additional measures or precautions as may be requisite. When sanitary reforms, requiring the sanction and co-operation of military authority, are urgently demanded, they will report at once, in writing, to the officer commanding corps, department, or division, the circumstances and necessities of the case, and the measures considered advisable for their relief, forwarding a duplicate of such reports to the Medical Inspector General.

They will instruct and direct the medical officers in charge as to the proper measures to be adopted for the correction of errors and abuses, and, in all cases of conflict of views, authority, or instructions, with those of medical directors, will report the circumstances fully and promptly to the Medical Inspector General for the Surgeon General's orders.

Upon or near the beginning of each month, medical inspectors will make minute and thorough inspections of hospitals, barracks, camps, transports, &c., &c., within the districts to which they are assigned, in conformity with these instructions, and the forms for inspection reports furnished them.

Monthly inspection reports, in addition to remarks under the several heads, will also convey the fullest information in regard to the medical and surgical treatment adopted; the advantages or disadvantages of location, construction, general arrangement and administration of hospitals, camps, barracks; the necessity for improvement, alteration, or repair, with such recommendations as will most certainly conduce to the health and comfort of the troops, and the proper care and treatment of the sick and wounded. When alterations, improvements, or repairs, requiring the action of heads of bureaus, are considered essential, special reports, accompanied by plans and approximate estimates of quantities or cost, will be made.

Medical inspectors will make themselves fully conversant with the regulations of the subsistence department in all that relates to issues to hospitals, whether general, field, division, or regimental, and will satisfy themselves, by rigid examination of accounts and expenditures, that the fund accruing from retained rations is judiciously applied, and not diverted from its proper purposes through the ignorance or inattention of medical officers, giving such information and instruction on this subject as may be required. They will also give close attention to the supervision of cooking by the medical officer, whose duty it is, under the act of Congress of March 3, 1863, and General Orders No. 247, of 1863, to "submit his suggestions for improving the cooking, in writing, to the commanding officer," and to accompany him in frequent inspections of the kitchens and messes.

They will exercise sound discrimination in reporting "an officer of the medical corps as disqualified, by age or otherwise, for promotion to a higher grade, or unfitted for the performance of his professional duties," and be prepared to submit evidence of its correctness to the medical board, by whom the charge will be investigated.

Medical inspectors are also charged with the duty of designating, to the surgeon in charge of general hospitals and convalescent camps, all soldiers who are in their opinion fit subjects for discharge on surgeons' certificate of disability, or sufficiently recovered to be able for duty. In all such cases they will direct the surgeon to discharge from service, in accordance with existing orders and regulations, or return to duty, those so designated.

Official communications to the Medical Inspector General will be directed to the Surgeon General United States army, and plainly addressed on the left-hand lower corner of envelope, "For the Medical Inspector General," the name and title of the writer being written under the words "Official Business."

It is expected that all commanding officers will afford every facility to medical inspectors in the execution of their important duties, giving such orders as may be necessary to carry into effect their suggestions and recommendations; and it is enjoined upon all medical officers, and others connected with the medical department of the United States army, to yield prompt compliance with the instructions they may receive from medical inspectors on duty in the army, department, or district in which they are serving, on all matters relating to the sanitary condition of the troops, and of the hygiene, police, discipline, and efficiency of hospitals.

By order of the Secretary of War:

E. D. TOWNSEND,
Assistant Adjutant General.

No. 5.

WAR DEPARTMENT, ADJUTANT GENERAL'S OFFICE,
Washington, January 28, 1863.

SIR: Your letter of the 12th of December last has been received, and I have respectfully to inform you that the following is the decision of the general-in-chief thereon : " Fort Scott is a permanent post."—(See General Orders No. 14, 1863.) The general hospital at a permanent post cannot, and ought not to, be independent of the post commander. General Orders No. 36 was framed to provide for hospitals established in cities and places not regularly garrisoned, where a state of things existed not provided for by any regulation.

The post commander should be held responsible that he does not interfere in the arrangement of the patients or of the hospital, further than may be necessary for the maintenance of proper discipline at his post. He should receive all soldiers not of his command who are discharged by the surgeon from the hospital as fit for duty, and should forward them to their companies under the orders of his department commander. He should also exercise the authority of "military commander" to indorse orders for discharge on the certificates of disability furnished by the hospital surgeon.

It is not for the post commander to say what patients shall be received in the hospital from distant commanders. The surgeon is responsible that the number is not excessive; and in this respect the Surgeon General of the United States army has direction over the hospitals. In all other points it is believed the army regulations are sufficient guide as to the relative duties of a commander of a post, and the surgeon in charge of a hospital thereat.

I am, sir, very respectfully, your obedient servant,

L. THOMAS, *Adjutant General.*

Major B. S. HENNING,
3d Wisconsin Cavalry, Commanding Fort Scott, Kansas.

Official :

E. D. TOWNSEND,
Assistant Adjutant General.

WAR DEPARTMENT,
Washington, D. C., August 5, 1863.

SIR: The attention of this department having been called to the establishment by you of United States general hospitals at Iowa City and Burlington, Iowa, the Secretary of War directs me to inform you that the establishment of these hospitals is unauthorized, is a needless expense to the government, and is therefore disapproved. If there are sick soldiers at the places indicated, the ordinary hospital accommodations organized with every command will suffice for their care. The Secretary directs me to call your attention to General Orders No. 36, of 1862, which places the general hospitals solely under the direction of the Surgeon General.

Very respectfully, your obedient servant,

JAMES A. HARDIE,
Assistant Adjutant General.

Brigadier General B. S. ROBERTS,
    United States Volunteers, Davenport, Iowa.

Official copy :

E. D. TOWNSEND,
Assistant Adjutant General.

SURGEON GENERAL'S OFFICE,
Washington City, D. C., August 20, 1863.

SIR: I have the honor to return herewith the letter of Brigadier General B. S. Roberts, referred to this office on the 20th instant for remark. In this letter Brigadier General Roberts asserts that certain instructions received by him from Major General Pope "are inoperative under an order the Surgeon General has sent Surgeon M. K. Taylor, in charge of hospital at Keokuk, directing him not to obey my orders," &c. These instructions of General Pope are, in substance, that certain patients at Keokuk and Dubuque hospitals, fit fof duty, be caused to rejoin their regiments. No orders conflicting with General Pope's instructions have ever been issued by this office. Some weeks since Brigadier General Roberts issued an order at variance with General Orders No. 36, of 1862, in directing hospitals to be established at two points where they were not needed, and at variance with General Orders No. 78, of 1862, in directing the transfer of convalescents thereto.

The Surgeon General directed Surgeon Taylor not to obey this order. General Roberts writes that this order of his was a "blind," as the soldiers transferred were sent to defend the provost marshal. If so, the men must have been presumed to be fit for duty, and the order of General Roberts sending such men from, rather than to their regiments, and not the order of the Surgeon General, rendered the instructions of General Pope inoperative.

I beg to call attention to an inaccuracy of Brigadier General Roberts in stating that the Surgeon General had directed Surgeon Taylor not to obey "his orders."

Upon receipt of General Roberts's order, above referred to, and after consultation with the Adjutant General of the army, and with his concurrence, Surgeon Taylor was directed by the Surgeon General not to obey "the order in reference to general hospitals at Burlington and Iowa City," in which Brigadier General Roberts attempted to interfere with affairs placed by the War Department beyond his control, and to saddle this department with unnecessary expense.

Very respectfully, your obedient servant,

JAMES R. SMITH,
Acting Surgeon General.

Brigadier General L. THOMAS,
  . *Adjutant General United States Army.*

Official copy :

E. D. TOWNSEND,
Assistant Adjutant General.

HEADQUARTERS DISTRICT OF IOWA,
Davenport, August 15, 1863.

COLONEL: I have the honor to ask your attention to the following extract from my letter of instructions from Major General Pope, commanding department of the northwest:

HEADQUARTERS DEPARTMENT OF THE NORTHWEST,
Milwaukie, June 9, 1863.

GENERAL: *   *   *   *   *   *   *   *

Your attention is called to the large hospitals at Keokuk and Dubuque. Many of the patients are so far convalescent as to be able to absent themselves habitually from the hospitals, and in one or two cases have committed outrages upon the citizens. In Keokuk this has been specially the case. You will please look into these matters to prevent a recurrence of them, and will take steps to insure the departure to join their regiments of all soldiers and officers capable of doing duty, it being assumed that such of them are fit for duty as are capable of absenting themselves from the hospitals, lounging about the streets, and attending places of amusement.   *   *   *   *   *.

I am, &c.,

JOHN POPE,
Major General Commanding.

These instructions are inoperative under an order the Surgeon General has sent Surgeon M. K. Taylor, in charge of hospital at Keokuk, directing him not to obey my orders, as well as by your letter of date of 11th of August, 1863, in which you say "you will revoke your order to Lieutenant Colonel Grier, as also any orders given by you to other officers who are acting under the special instructions of the War Department, or who have not been properly placed under your orders."

Is it the intention of your letter to take away from me the supervision of hospitals, as instructed by General Pope?

I am, sir, very respectfully, your obedient servant,

B. S. ROBERTS,
Brigadier General Volunteers.

Colonel E. D. TOWNSEND,
Assistant Adjutant General U. S. A., Washington.

Official copy: E. D. TOWNSEND,
Assistant Adjutant General.

[Telegram.]

SURGEON GENERAL'S OFFICE,
Washington City, D. C., August 1, 1863.

You will not obey the order you have received from General Roberts, in reference to general hospitals at Burlington and Iowa. The War Department has decided that general hospitals are under me, and I will not pay any expenses connected with hospitals established without my authority.

The transfer of soldiers to other hospitals is also under my direction. You will not make the transfer ordered to Burlington or Iowa City.

W. A. HAMMOND,
Surgeon General.

Surgeon M. K. TAYLOR,
United States Volunteers, Keokuk, Iowa.

WAR DEPARTMENT, ADJUTANT GENERAL'S OFFICE,
Washington, December 31, 1863.

SIR: The communication of Surgeon John T. Carpenter, United States volunteers, under date of 22d instant, in relation to the conduct of Brigadier General Brayman, commanding Camp Dennison, Ohio, with respect to the company of the Invalid corps ordered as a guard at the general hospital, and requesting that orders be given to restrain the post commander from interference with the management of the general hospital, has been submitted to the general-in-chief, who directs me to say, in reply, that Brigadier General Brayman has no right to interfere with the management of the hospital, but that his duties in reference to the troops that may come within the line of his command are those of a commanding officer of a military post, and that he should, therefore, have control of the company of the Invalid corps, furnished to preserve discipline and good order at the hospital.

I am, sir, very respectfully, your obedient servant,

E. D. TOWNSEND,
Assistant Adjutant General.

Colonel J. K. BARNES,
Acting Surgeon General.

Official copy:

E. D. TOWNSEND,
Assistant Adjutant General.

WAR DEPARTMENT, ADJUTANT GENERAL'S OFFICE,
Washington, January 29, 1864.

SIR: The communication of Surgeon Adolph, major U. S. volunteers, dated St. Augustine, Florida, December 11, 1863, reporting that he had arrested First Lieutenant and Adjutant Edward Millard, 117th New York volunteers, a convalescent officer under his care, with the accompanying papers in the case, has been submitted to the general-in-chief, who directs me to reply as follows:

"General Orders No. 36, of 1862, place the general hospitals under the direction of the Surgeon General. The military commander is not to interfere with the management of the hospitals. He controls such guards as may be furnished to preserve discipline and good order at the military hospitals, and his duties in reference to all troops who are within the limits of his command are those of a commanding officer of a military post. This, it would appear, designates him as the proper authority to make arrests. Surgeons in charge of general hospitals are not recognized as commanding officers in the sense of paragraph 221, Revised Army Regulations.

"In case of conduct prejudicial to good order, &c., &c., the surgeon in charge has his remedy by preferring charges to the military commander, if there is one on the spot; if not, to the department commander."

The decision of Captain Henshaw, acting judge advocate, is concurred in.

I am, sir, very respectfully, your obedient servant,

E. D. TOWNSEND,
Assistant Adjutant General.

Major General Q. A. GILLMORE,
Commanding Department of the South,
Folly Island, South Carolina.

Official copy:

E. D. TOWNSEND,
Assistant Adjutant General.

HEADQUARTERS DEPARTMENT OF THE SOUTH,
Judge Advocate's Office, Folly Island, S. C., December 16, 1863.

SIR: The communication of Surgeon Adolph, major U. S. volunteers, dated St. Augustine, Florida, December 11, 1863, stating that he had arrested First Lieutenant and Adjutant Edward Millard, 117th New York volunteers, (a convalescent officer under his care,) upon charges to be duly preferred, and inquiring as to the right of a surgeon to arrest an officer in such cases, having been referred to this office, I have the honor to reply :

That paragraph 221, Revised Army Regulations of 1863, is conclusive upon this question. The commanding officer referred to is the senior officer in command of the troops or station.

In this case, therefore, it appears that Colonel F. A. Osborne, 24th Massachusetts volunteers, was the proper officer to make the arrest.

Very respectfully, your obedient servant,
JOHN C. HENSHAW,
Acting Judge Advocate.

Brigadier General J. W. TURNER,
Chief of Staff, Headquarters Department of the South.

HEADQUARTERS DEPARTMENT OF THE SOUTH,
Folly Island, S. C., December 17, 1863.

Official :
E. W. SMITH,
Assistant Adjutant General.

Official :
THOMAS F. EDWARDS,
Lieutenant and Post Adjutant.

Official copy :
E. D. TOWNSEND,
Assistant Adjutant General.

Ex. Doc. 21——5

www.ingramcontent.com/pod-product-compliance
Lightning Source LLC
Chambersburg PA
CBHW031321280626
47169CB00019B/2570